"In one b ... not propo... you say that you find me attractive."

"Actually, my comment was more objective than subjective," Michael told her. "But while I do think you're a very attractive woman, I didn't hire you in order to pursue a personal relationship with you."

"Okay," Hannah said, still sounding wary.

Not that he could blame her. Because even as he was saying one thing, he was thinking something else entirely.

"In fact, I wouldn't have invited you to spend the summer here if I thought there was any danger of an attraction leading to anything else."

"Okay," she said again.

"I just want you to understand that I didn't intend for this to happen at all," he said.

And then he kissed her.

Dear Reader,

It has been a sincere pleasure to return to the island paradise of Tesoro del Mar, to revisit some familiar characters and introduce some new ones. Hannah Castillo is one of the new characters you'll meet in *Prince Daddy & the Nanny*.

After the death of her mother when Hannah was only eight years old, her father sent her to Tesoro del Mar to live with her uncle Phillip, the royal physician. Eighteen years later, when Hannah takes a summer job looking after widowed Prince Michael's four-year-old daughter, she can't help but see parallels between the princess's lonely childhood and her own. As she works to help bridge the gap between father and daughter, Hannah finds herself falling for both of them and wishing that the summer would never end.

But of course, Hannah knows that the idea of a prince loving a commoner is nothing more than a fairy tale, and fairy tales don't come true. Except, maybe, in Tesoro del Mar....

I hope you enjoy Hannah's story.

Best,

Brenda Harlen

PRINCE DADDY & THE NANNY

BRENDA HARLEN

Harlequin®

SPECIAL EDITION

Recycling programs
for this product may
not exist in your area.

ISBN-13: 978-0-373-65629-5

PRINCE DADDY & THE NANNY

Copyright © 2011 by Brenda Harlen

Printed in U.S.A.

Recent books by Brenda Harlen

Harlequin Special Edition

†*Prince Daddy & the Nanny* #2147

Silhouette Special Edition

Once and Again #1714
*Her Best-Kept Secret #1756
The Marriage Solution #1811
**One Man's Family #1827
The New Girl in Town #1859
†*The Prince's Royal Dilemma* #1898
†*The Prince's Cowgirl Bride* #1920
^*Family in Progress* #1928
†*The Prince's Holiday Baby* #1942
‡*The Texas Tycoon's Christmas Baby* #2016
‡‡*The Engagement Project* #2021
‡‡*The Pregnancy Plan* #2038
‡‡*The Baby Surprise* #2056
~*Thunder Canyon Homecoming* #2079
†*The Prince's Second Chance* #2100

Romantic Suspense

McIver's Mission #1224
Some Kind of Hero #1246
Extreme Measures #1282
Bulletproof Hearts #1313
Dangerous Passions #1394

*Family Business
**Logan's Legacy Revisited
†Reigning Men
††Back in Business
‡The Foleys and the McCords
‡‡Brides and Babies
~Montana Mavericks:
  Thunder Canyon Cowboys

BRENDA HARLEN

grew up in a small town, surrounded by books and imaginary friends. Although she always dreamed of being a writer, she chose to follow a more traditional career path first. After two years of practicing as an attorney (including an appearance in front of the Supreme Court of Canada), she gave up her "real" job to be a mom and to try her hand at writing books. Three years, five manuscripts and another baby later, she sold her first book—an RWA Golden Heart winner—to Silhouette Books.

Brenda lives in southern Ontario with her real-life husband/hero, two heroes-in-training and two neurotic dogs. She is still surrounded by books (too many books, according to her children) and imaginary friends, but she also enjoys communicating with real people. Readers can contact Brenda by email at brendaharlen@yahoo.com or by snail mail c/o Harlequin Books, 233 Broadway, Suite 1001, New York, NY 10279.

To Kate Weichelt—
who has helped brainstorm solutions to many story
problems over the years, including a few in this one.

Thanks for being a friend, an inspiration,
and especially for being you!

Chapter One

So this is how the other half lives.

Hannah Castillo's eyes widened as she drove through the gates into the upscale neighborhood of Verde Colinas.

Actually, she knew it was more likely how half of one percent of the population lived, and she couldn't help wondering what it would be like to grow up in a place like this. Having spent the first eight years of her life moving from village to village with her missionary parents, she hadn't realized there was anything different until her uncle Phillip had brought her to his home in Tesoro del Mar.

And even then, she wouldn't have imagined that there was anything like *this*. She hadn't known that real people lived in such luxury. Not regular people, of course, but billionaires and business tycoons, musicians and movie stars, philanthropists and princes. Well, at least one prince.

Prince Michael Leandres was the thirty-eight-year-old president of a multimedia advertising company, cousin of the prince regent, widowed father of Tesoro del Mar's youngest princess, and the first man who had ever made her heart go pitter-patter.

As she slowed to wait for another set of gates to open so that she could enter the drive that led to the prince's home, she couldn't help but smile at the memory. She'd been twelve at the time, and as flustered as she was flattered when Uncle Phillip asked her to accompany him to the by-invitation-only Gala Opening of the Port Augustine Art Gallery.

She'd been so preoccupied thinking about what she would wear (she would have to get a new dress, because a gala event surely required a gown) and whether she might be allowed to wear makeup (at least a little bit of eyeliner and a touch of lip gloss) that she hadn't given a thought to the other guests who might be in attendance at the event. And then she'd walked through the doors on her uncle's arm and spotted Prince Michael.

To a preteen girl who was just starting to take note of the male species, he was a full six feet of masculine perfection. He was also a dozen years older than she, and already there were rumors swirling about his plans to marry his longtime sweetheart, Samantha Chandelle. But Hannah's enamored heart hadn't cared. She'd been content to admire him from afar, her blood racing through her veins just because he was in the same room with her.

Since then, she'd met a lot of other men, dated some of them and even had intimate relationships with a few. But not one of them had ever made her feel the same kind of pulse-pounding, spine-tingling excitement that she'd felt simply by being in the presence of Prince Michael—not even Harrison Parker, the earl who had been her fiancé for a short time.

Now, fourteen years after her first meeting with the prince, she was going to come face-to-face with him again. She might even have a conversation with him—if she could manage to untie her tongue long enough to form any coherent words—and hopefully persuade him that she was the perfect woman to take care of his adorable daughter. Of course, it might be easier to convince him if she believed it herself, but truthfully, she wasn't sure how she'd let Uncle Phillip convince *her* that the idea of working as a nanny for the summer wasn't a completely ridiculous one.

Or maybe she did know. Maybe it was as simple as the fact that she was in desperate need of an income and a place to stay for the summer, and working as a nanny at Cielo del Norte—a royal estate on the northern coast—would provide her with both. But on top of that, her uncle claimed that he "would be most grateful" if she would at least meet with the prince—as if it would be doing him some kind of favor, which made the request impossible for Hannah to deny. That the salary the prince was offering was more than enough to finally pay off the last of her student loans was a bonus.

As for responsibilities, she would be providing primary care for the widowed prince's almost-four-year-old daughter. She didn't figure that should be too difficult for someone with a master's degree, but still her stomach was twisted in knots of both excitement and apprehension as she turned her ancient secondhand compact into the winding drive that led toward the prince's home.

Having grown up in tents and mud huts and, on very rare occasions, bedding down on an actual mattress in a cheap hotel room, she was unprepared for life in Tesoro del Mar. When she moved into her uncle's home, she had not just a bed but a whole room to herself. She had clothes in an actual closet, books on a shelf and a hot meal on the table every night. It took her a long time to get used to living in such luxurious surroundings, but pulling up in front of the prince's home now, she knew she was about to discover the real definition of luxury.

The hand-carved double front doors were opened by a uniformed butler who welcomed her into a spacious marble-tiled foyer above which an enormous crystal chandelier was suspended. As she followed him down a long hallway, their footsteps muted by the antique Aubusson carpet, she noted the paintings on the walls. She had enough knowledge of and appreciation for art to recognize that the works that hung in gilded frames were not reproductions but original pieces by various European masters.

The butler led her through an open doorway and into what was apparently the prince's office. Prince Michael himself was seated behind a wide desk. Bookcases filled with leather-bound volumes lined the wall behind him. The adjoining wall boasted floor-to-ceiling windows set off by textured velvet curtains. It even smelled rich, she thought, noting the scents of lemon polish, aged leather and fresh flowers.

"Miss Castillo, Your Highness." The butler announced her presence in a formal tone, then bowed as he retreated from the room.

The nerves continued to twist and knot in her stomach. Was she supposed to bow? Curtsy? She should have asked her uncle about the appropriate etiquette, but she'd had so many other questions and concerns about his proposition that the intricacies of royal protocol had never crossed her mind.

She debated for about ten seconds, then realized the prince hadn't looked away from his computer screen long enough to even glance in her direction. She could have bowed *and* curtsied *and* done a tap dance and he wouldn't even have noticed. Instead, she focused on her breathing and tried to relax, reminding herself that Michael Leandres might be a prince, but he was still just a man.

Then he pushed away from his desk and rose to his feet, and she realized that she was wrong.

This man wasn't "just" anything. He was taller than she'd remembered, broader across the shoulders and so much more handsome in person than he appeared in newspaper photos and on magazine covers. And her heart, already racing, leaped again.

He gestured to the chairs in front of his desk. "Please, have a seat."

His voice was deep and cultured, and with each word, little tingles danced over her skin. She couldn't be sure if her reaction to him was that of a girl so long enamored of a prince or of a woman instinctively responding to an undeniably attractive man, but she did know that it was wholly inappropriate under the circumstances. She was here to interview for a job, not ogle the man, she sternly reminded herself as she lowered herself into the Queen Anne–style chair and murmured, "Thank you."

"I understand that you're interested in working as my daughter's nanny for the summer," the prince said without further preamble.

"I am," she agreed, then felt compelled to add, "although I have to confess that I've never actually worked as a nanny before."

He nodded, seemingly unconcerned by this fact. "Your uncle told me that you're a teacher."

"That's correct."

"How long have you been teaching?"

"Six years," she told him.

"Do you enjoy it?"

"Of course," she agreed.

He frowned, and she wondered if her response was somehow the wrong one. But then she realized that his gaze had dropped to the BlackBerry on his desk. He punched a few buttons before he looked up at her again.

"And I understand that you've met Riley," he prompted.

"Only once, a few months ago. I was with a friend at the art gallery—" coincidentally, the same art gallery where she'd first seen him so many years earlier, though it was unlikely that he had any recollection of that earlier meeting "—and Princess Riley was there with her nanny."

Phillip had explained to her that the nanny—Brigitte Francoeur—had been caring for the princess since she was a baby, and that Prince Michael had been having more difficulty than he'd anticipated in his efforts to find a replacement for the woman who was leaving his employ to get married.

"The way Brigitte told it to me was that my daughter ran away from her, out of the café—and straight into you, dumping her ice cream cone into your lap."

Hannah waited, wondering about the relevance of his recounting of the event.

"I kept expecting to read about it in the paper," he explained. *"Princess Riley Accosts Museum Guest with Scoop of Strawberry."*

She couldn't help but smile. "I'm sure, even if there had been reporters in the vicinity, they would not have found the moment newsworthy, Your Highness."

"I've learned, over the years, that a public figure doesn't only need to worry about the legitimate media but anyone who feels they have a story to tell. A lot of ordinary citizens would have happily sold that little tale to *El Informador* for a tidy sum. Not only did you not run to the press to sell the story of the out-of-control princess, but you bought her a new ice cream cone to replace the one she'd lost."

"It wasn't her fault that the strawberry went splat," she said lightly.

"A gracious interpretation of the event," he noted. "And one that gives me hope you might finally be someone who could fill the hole that Brigitte's absence will leave in Riley's life."

"For the summer, you mean," Hannah sought to clarify.

"For the summer," he agreed. "Although I was originally hoping to find a permanent replacement, the situation has changed. The current nanny is leaving at the end of this week to finalize preparations for her wedding, and my daughter and I are scheduled to be at Cielo del Norte by the beginning of next. None of the applicants I've interviewed have been suitable, and your uncle has managed to convince me to settle for an interim solution to the problem."

She wasn't sure if she should be amused or insulted. "Is that why I'm here? Am I—"

"Excuse me," he interrupted, picking up the BlackBerry again. He frowned as he read the message, then typed a quick response. "You were saying?" he prompted when he was done.

"I was wondering if I'm supposed to be your 'interim solution.'"

His lips curved, just a little, in response to her dry tone. "I hope so. Although my royal duties are minimal, my responsibilities to my business are not," he explained. "I spend the summers at Cielo del Norte because it is a tradition that began when Samantha—"

His hesitation was brief, but the shadows that momentarily clouded his dark eyes confirmed her uncle's suspicion that the prince was still grieving for the wife he'd lost only hours after the birth of their daughter, and Hannah's heart couldn't help but ache for a man who would have faced such an indescribable loss so quickly on the heels of intense joy.

"—when Samantha and I first got married. A tradition that she wanted to carry on with our children." He cleared his throat, dropping his gaze to reshuffle some papers on his desk. "But the truth is that I still have a company to run. Thankfully I can do that from the beach almost as easily as I can do it from my office downtown. I just need to know that Riley is in good hands so that I can focus on what I need to do."

Be a good girl and stay out of the way so that Daddy can do his work.

The words, long forgotten, echoed in the back of Hannah's mind and sliced through her heart.

Maybe they had been born into completely different worlds, but Hannah suddenly wondered if she and Princess Riley might have a lot more in common than she ever would have suspected.

Her own father had rarely had any time for her, and then, when she was eight years old, her mother had died. She still felt the void in her heart. She still missed her. And she wanted to believe that in some small way, she might be able to fill that void for the prince's daughter. If he would give her the chance.

"Are you offering me the job, Your Highness?" she asked him now.

"Yes, I am," he affirmed with a nod.

"Then I accept."

Michael knew he should be relieved. He'd needed to hire a nanny for the summer, and now he'd done so. But there was something about Hannah Castillo that made him uneasy. Or maybe he was simply regretting the fact that his daughter would have to say goodbye to her long-term caregiver. Brigitte had been a constant in Riley's life almost from the very beginning, and he knew it would take his daughter some time to adjust to her absence.

He wished he could believe that being at Cielo del Norte with him would give Riley comfort, but the truth was, his daughter was much closer to her nanny than she was to her father. It was a truth that filled him with grief and regret, but a truth nonetheless.

He and Sam had long ago agreed that they would both play an active role in raising their child. Of course, that agreement had been made before Sam died, so soon after giving birth to their baby girl. How was one man supposed to care for an infant daughter, grieve for the wife he'd lost and continue to run the company they'd built together?

It hadn't taken him long to realize that there was no way that he could do it on his own, so he'd hired Brigitte. She'd been a child studies student at the local university who Sam had interviewed as a potential mother's helper when the expectation was that his wife would be around to raise their daughter.

For the first couple years, Brigitte had tended to Riley during the day and continued her studies at night, with Michael's sister, Marissa, taking over the baby's care after-hours. Then when Brigitte finished university and Michael's sister took on additional responsibilities elsewhere, the young woman had become Riley's full-time nanny.

I don't want our child raised by a series of nannies.

Sam's voice echoed in the back of his mind, so clearly that he almost expected to turn around and see her standing there.

He understood why she'd felt that way and he'd shared her concerns, but he convinced himself that a wonderful and energetic caregiver like Brigitte was the exception to the rule. She certainly wasn't like any of the harsh disciplinarians who had been hired to ensure that he and his siblings grew up to become proper royals.

Still, he knew his failure wasn't in hiring Brigitte—or even in hiring Hannah Castillo. His failure was in abdicating his own responsibilities as a father.

He'd wanted to do more, to be more involved in Riley's life. But the first few months after Sam's death had been a blur. He'd barely been able to focus on getting up every morning, never mind putting a diaper on a baby, so those tasks had fallen to Brigitte or Marissa.

At six months of age, Riley had broken through the veil of grief that had surrounded him. He'd been drinking his morning coffee and scanning the headlines of the newspaper when Marissa had carried her into the kitchen. He'd glanced up, and when he did, the little girl's big brown eyes widened. "Da!" she said, and clapped her hands.

He didn't know enough about a baby's developmental milestones to know that she was speaking her first word several months ahead of schedule. All he knew was that the single word and the smile on her face completely melted his heart.

Sam had given him the precious gift of this baby girl, and somehow he had missed most of the first six months of her life. He vowed then and there to make more of an effort, to spend more time with her, to make sure she knew how much she was loved. But he was still awkward with her—she was so tiny and delicate, and he felt so big and clumsy whenever he held her. Thankfully, she was tolerant of his ineptitude, and her smiles and giggles gave him confidence and comfort.

And then, shortly after Riley's second birthday, Brigitte made a discovery. Riley had been an early talker—not just speaking a few words or occasional phrases but in complete sentences—and she often repeated the words when the nanny read her a story. But on this particular day, Brigitte opened a book that they'd never read before, and Riley began to read the words without any help or prompting.

A few months after that, Brigitte had been playing in the music room with the little girl, showing her how she could make sounds by pressing down on the piano's ivory keys, and Riley had quickly started to put the sounds together to make music.

Before she turned three, Riley had been examined by more doctors and teachers than Michael could count, and the results had been unequivocal—his daughter was intellectually gifted.

He was proud, of course, and more than a little baffled. As if he hadn't struggled enough trying to relate to the tiny little person when he'd believed that she was a normal child, learning that she was of superior intelligence made him worry all the more. Thankfully, Brigitte had known what to do. She'd met with specialists and interviewed teachers and made all of the arrangements to ensure that Riley's talents were being nurtured. And when the advertising company he and Sam had established ran into difficulties because an associate stole several key clients, Michael refocused his attention on the business, confident his daughter was in much more capable hands than his own.

It had taken a while, but the business was finally back on solid ground, Riley was happy and healthy, Brigitte was getting married and moving to Iceland, and he had a new nanny for the summer.

So why was he suddenly worried that hiring Hannah Castillo had set him upon a path that would change his life?

He didn't want anything to change. He was content with the status quo. Maybe it wasn't what he'd envisioned for his life half a dozen years earlier, and maybe there was an empty place in his heart since Samantha had died, but he knew that he could never fill that void. Because there would never be anyone he would love as he'd loved Sam. There was no way anyone else could ever take her place.

Each day that had passed in the years since Sam's death had cemented that conviction. He had no difficulty turning away from the flirtatious glances that were sent in his direction, and even the more blatant invitations did nothing to stir his interest.

Then Hannah Castillo had walked into his office and he'd felt a definite stir of...something.

The morning weather reports had warned of a storm on the horizon, and he'd tried to convince himself that the change in the weather was responsible for the crackle in the air. But he knew that there was no meteorological explanation for the jolt that went through his system when he'd taken the hand she offered, no logical reason for the rush of blood through his veins when she smiled at him.

And he'd felt an uneasiness in the pit of his belly, a tiny suspicion that maybe hiring a young, attractive woman as his daughter's temporary nanny wasn't the best idea he'd ever had.

Because as much as he'd kept the tone of the interview strictly professional, he hadn't failed to notice that the doctor's niece was quite beautiful. She wasn't very tall—probably not more than five feet four inches without the two-inch heels on her feet. And while the tailored pants and matching jacket she wore weren't provocative by any stretch of the imagination, they failed to disguise her distinctly feminine curves. Her honey-blond hair had been scraped away from her face and secured in a tight knot at the back of her head in a way that might have made her look prim, but the effect was softened by warm blue eyes and sweetly shaped lips that were quick to smile.

Even as he'd offered her the job, he'd wondered if he was making a mistake. But he'd reassured himself that it was only for two months.

Now that she was gone and he was thinking a little more clearly, he suspected that it was going to be a very long summer.

Chapter Two

Hannah went through her closet, tossing items into one of two separate piles on her bed. The first was for anything she might need at Cielo del Norte, and the other was for everything else, which would go into storage. Thankfully, she didn't have a lot of stuff, but she still had to sort and pack everything before she handed over her keys, and the task was much more time-consuming than she would have imagined.

Subletting her apartment had seemed like a good idea when she'd planned to spend the summer in China as an ESL teacher. Unfortunately the job offer had fallen through when she'd declined to share a tiny one-bedroom apartment with the coworker who'd made it clear that he wanted her in his bed. She felt like such a fool. She should have realized that Ian had ulterior motives when he first offered to take her to China, but she honestly hadn't had a clue.

Yes, they'd been dating for a few months, but only casually and certainly not exclusively. When she'd sidestepped his advances, he'd seemed to accept that she didn't want to take their relationship to the next level. So when he'd presented her with the opportunity to teach in China during the summer break, she'd trusted that he was making the offer as a colleague and a professional. Finding out that he expected them to share an apartment put a different spin on things.

Ian's ultimatum was further evidence that she had poor judgment with respect to romantic entanglements, a truth first revealed by her broken engagement three years earlier. Now she had additionial confirmation in the fact that she was fighting an attraction to a man who wasn't just a prince but grieving the death of his wife. With a sigh, Hannah taped up yet another box and pushed it aside.

When she finished in the bedroom, she packed up the contents of the bathroom. By the time she got to the kitchen, her legs were protesting all the bending and her shoulders were aching from all the lifting. But she still had to empty the pantry of boxed food and canned goods, which she was in the process of doing when the downstairs buzzer sounded.

She stopped packing only long enough to press the button that released the exterior door locks. It was six o'clock on a Friday night, so she knew it was her uncle Phillip at the door. Weekly dinners had become their way of keeping in touch when Hannah moved out of his house, and she sincerely regretted that she would have to skip the ritual for the next couple of months.

"It's unlocked," she said in response to his knock.

"A woman living alone in the city should lock her doors," her uncle chided, passing through the portal with a large flat box in his hand and the sweet and spicy aroma of sausage pizza enveloping him. "Didn't I ever teach you that?"

"You tried to teach me so many things," she teased, standing up and wiping her hands on her jeans. "I thought I'd seen more than enough boxes today, but that one just changed my mind."

"Packing is hard work." He set the pizza on the counter

and gave her a quick hug. He smelled of clean soap with subtle hints of sandalwood—a scent that was as warm and dependable as everything else about him.

"I'm almost done." She moved out of his embrace to retrieve plates from the cupboard. "Finally."

"How long have you been at it?" He opened the refrigerator, pulled a couple of cans of soda from the nearly empty shelves.

"It seems like forever. Probably about seven hours. But I've already moved a lot of stuff into a storage locker downstairs, so it shouldn't take me too much longer."

Hannah took a seat on the opposite side of the table from him and helped herself to a slice of pizza. She hadn't realized how hungry she was until she took the first bite. Of course, she'd been too nervous about her interview with Prince Michael to eat lunch earlier, which reminded her that she hadn't yet told her uncle about the new job.

But he spoke before she could, saying, "I heard you're heading up to Cielo del Norte on Monday."

Phillip was a highly regarded doctor in the community and his network of contacts was legendary, but she still didn't see how he could have learned the outcome of her interview with the prince already. "How did you hear that?"

He smiled, recognizing the pique in her tone. "The prince called to thank me for the recommendation."

"Oh." She should have considered that possibility. "Well, his appreciation might be a little premature."

"I have every confidence that you're just what his daughter needs," Phillip said.

She wasn't so sure. She was a teacher, and she loved being a teacher, but that didn't mean she was qualified to work as a nanny.

And yet that wasn't her greatest worry. A far bigger concern, and one she was reluctant to admit even to herself, was that she now knew she'd never completely let go of her childhood infatuation with Prince Michael Leandres.

She should have outgrown that silly crush years ago. And she'd thought she had—until she stood in front of him with her heart beating so loudly inside of her chest she was amazed that he couldn't hear it.

So now she was trying *not* to think about the fact that she would be spending the next two months at Cielo del Norte with the sexy prince who was still grieving the loss of his wife, and attempting to focus instead on the challenges of spending her days with an almost-four-year-old princess.

"I wish I shared your faith," Hannah said to her uncle now.

"Why would you have doubts?"

"I'm just not sure that hiring a temporary replacement is the best thing for a young child who has just lost her primary caregiver." It was the only concern she felt comfortable offering her uncle, because she knew that confiding in him about her childhood crush would only worry him.

"Your compassion is only one of the reasons I know you'll be perfect for the job," Phillip said. "As for Riley, I think she'll surprise you. She is remarkably mature for her age and very well-adjusted."

"Then why does the prince even need a nanny? Why can't he just enjoy a summer at the beach with his daughter without pawning off the responsibility of her care on someone else?"

"Prince Michael is doing the best that he can," her uncle said. "He's had to make a lot of adjustments in his life, too, since losing his wife."

Hannah used to wonder why people referred to a death as a loss—as if the person was only missing. She'd been there when her mother died, so she knew that she wasn't "lost" but gone. Forever.

And after her death her husband had handed their daughter over to his brother-in-law, happy to relinquish to someone else the responsibility of raising his only child. Just as the prince was doing.

Was she judging him too harshly? Possibly. Certainly she was judging him prematurely. There were a lot of professionals who hired caregivers for their children, and although Prince Michael kept a fairly low profile in comparison to other members of his family, she knew that he had occasional royal duties to perform in addition to being president and CEO of his own company. And he was a widower trying to raise a young daughter on his own after the unexpected death of his wife from severe hypoglycemia only hours after childbirth.

Maybe her uncle was right and he was doing the best that he could. In any event, she would be at Cielo del Norte in a few days with the prince and his daughter. No doubt her questions would be answered then.

"So what are you going to do with your Friday nights while I'm gone this summer?" she asked her uncle, hoping a change in the topic of conversation would also succeed in changing the direction of her thoughts.

"I'm sure there will be occasional medical emergencies to keep me occupied," Phillip told her.

She smiled, because she knew it was true. "Will you come to visit me?"

"If I can get away. But you really shouldn't worry about me—there's enough going on with the Juno project at the hospital to keep me busy over the next several months."

"Okay, I won't worry," she promised. "But I will miss you."

"You'll be too busy rubbing elbows with royalty to think about anyone else," he teased.

She got up to clear their empty plates away, not wanting him to see the flush in her cheeks. Because the idea of rubbing anything of hers against anything of Prince

Michael's—even something as innocuous as elbows—made her feel hot and tingly inside.

Heading up to Cielo del Norte on Saturday afternoon had seemed like a good idea to Michael while he was packing up the car. And Riley had been excited to start their summer vacation. Certainly she'd given him no reason to anticipate any problems, but if there was one thing he should have learned by now about parenting, it was to always expect the unexpected.

The trip itself had been uneventful enough. Estavan Fuentes, the groundskeeper and general maintenance man, had been waiting when they arrived to unload the vehicle; and Caridad, Estavan's wife and the longtime housekeeper of the estate, had the beds all made up and dinner ready in the oven.

As Michael had enjoyed a glass of his favorite cabernet along with the hot meal, he'd felt the tensions of the city melt away. It was several hours later before he recognized that peaceful interlude as the calm before the storm.

Now it was after midnight, and as he slipped out onto the back terrace and into the blissful quiet of the night, he exhaled a long, weary sigh. It was the only sound aside from the rhythmic lap of the waves against the shore in the distance, and he took a moment to absorb—and appreciate—the silence.

With another sigh, he sank onto the end of a lounge chair and let the peacefulness of the night settle like a blanket across his shoulders. Tipping his head back, he marveled at the array of stars that sparkled like an exquisite selection of diamonds spread out on a black jeweler's cloth.

He jolted when he heard the French door slide open again.

"Relax—she's sleeping like a baby." His sister's voice was little more than a whisper, as if she was also reluctant to disturb the quiet.

He settled into his chair again. "I thought you'd be asleep, too. You said you wanted to get an early start back in the morning."

"I do," Marissa agreed. "But the stars were calling to me."

He smiled, remembering that those were the same words their father used to say whenever they found him out on this same terrace late at night. They'd spent a lot of time at Cielo del Norte when they were kids, and Michael had a lot of fond memories of their family vacations, particularly in the earlier years, before their father passed away. Their mother had continued the tradition for a while, but it was never the same afterward and they all knew it.

Gaetan Leandres had been raised with a deep appreciation for not just the earth but the seas and the skies, too. He'd been a farmer by trade and a stargazer by choice. He'd spent hours sitting out here, searching for various constellations and pointing them out to his children. He'd once told Michael that whenever he felt overwhelmed by earthly burdens, he just had to look up at the sky and remember how much bigger the world was in comparison to his problems.

Marissa sat down on the end of a lounger, her gaze on something far off in the distance. "I know they're the same stars I can see from my windows in the city, but they look so different out here. So much brighter."

"Why don't you stay for a few days?" he offered, feeling more than a little guilty that she'd driven all the way from Port Augustine in response to his distress call.

"I wish I could, but I've got three full days of meetings scheduled this week."

"Which you should have told me when I got you on the phone."

She lifted a shoulder. "I couldn't not come, not when I heard Riley sobbing in the background."

And that was why he'd called. His daughter, tired from

the journey, had fallen asleep earlier than usual. A few hours later, she'd awakened screaming like a banshee and nothing he said or did seemed to console her. She'd been in an unfamiliar bed in an unfamiliar room and Brigitte—her primary caregiver—was on a plane halfway to Iceland. Michael had tried to console Riley, he'd cuddled her, rocked her, put on music for her to listen to, tried to read stories to her, but nothing had worked.

It hadn't occurred to him to call his mother—the princess royal wouldn't know what to do any more than he did. It wasn't in her nature to offer comfort or support. In fact, the only things he'd ever been able to count on his mother to do were interfere and manipulate. So he'd picked up the phone and dialed his sister's number. During the first year and a half after Sam's death, before he'd hired Brigitte full-time, Marissa had been there, taking care of both him and his daughter. And, once again, she'd come through when he needed her.

"Do you think I should have stayed in Port Augustine with her?" he asked his sister now.

"That would have meant a much shorter trip for me," she teased, "but no. I'm glad you're maintaining the family tradition."

Except that he didn't have a family anymore—for the past four summers, it had been just him and Riley. And Brigitte, of course.

"When does the new nanny arrive?"

Marissa's question drew him back to the present—and to more immediate concerns.

"Tomorrow."

She tilted her head. "Why do you sound wary?"

"Do I?" he countered.

"Are you having second thoughts about her qualifications?"

"No," he said, then reconsidered his response. "Yes."

Her brows rose.

No, because it wasn't anything on Hannah's résumé that gave him cause for concern. Yes, because he wasn't completely convinced that a teacher would be a suitable caregiver for his daughter—even on a temporary basis.

"No," he decided. "Dr. Marotta would never have recommended her if he didn't believe she was capable of caring for Riley."

"Of course not," his sister agreed. "So what are you worried about?"

He didn't say anything. He didn't even deny that he was worried, because his sister knew him too well to believe it. Worse, she would probably see right through the lie to the true origin of his concern. And he was concerned, mostly about the fact that he'd been thinking of Hannah Castillo far too frequently since their first meeting.

He'd had no preconceptions when he'd agreed to interview her. His only concern had been to find someone suitable to oversee the care of his daughter during the summer—because after conducting more than a dozen interviews, he'd been shocked to realize how *un*suitable so many of the applicants had been.

Almost half of them he'd automatically rejected because of their advanced age. Logically, he knew that was unfair, but he had too many unhappy memories of strict, gray-haired disciplinarians from his own childhood. Another few he'd disregarded when it became apparent that they were more interested in flirting with him than caring for his daughter. Two more had been shown the door when they'd been caught snapping photos of his home with the cameras on their cell phones.

At the conclusion of those interviews, he'd almost given up hope of finding a replacement for Brigitte. Then, during a casual conversation with Riley's doctor, he'd mentioned his dilemma and Phillip had suggested that his niece might be interested in the job—but only for the summer.

So Michael had agreed to interview her and crossed his fingers that she would be suitable. Then Hannah had walked into his office, and *suitable* was the last thought on his mind.

"Oh," Marissa said, and sat back, a smile playing at the corners of her lips.

He scowled. "What is that supposed to mean?"

"She's very attractive, isn't she?"

His scowl deepened.

"I should have guessed. Nothing ever flusters you—okay, nothing except anything to do with Riley," she clarified. "But this woman has you completely flustered."

"I am not flustered," he denied.

"This is good," Marissa continued as if he hadn't spoken. "And it's time."

"Mar—"

She put her hands up in a gesture of surrender. "Okay, okay. I won't push for any details."

"There are no details," he insisted.

"Not yet," she said, and smiled.

His sister always liked to get in the last word, and this time he let her. It would serve no purpose to tell her that he wasn't interested in any kind of relationship with Riley's temporary nanny—it only mattered that it was true.

And he would repeat it to himself as many times as necessary until he actually believed it.

With every mile that Hannah got closer to Cielo del Norte, her excitement and apprehension increased. If she'd been nervous before her previous meeting with the prince— simply at the thought of meeting him—that was nothing compared to the tension that filled her now. Because now she was actually going to live with him—and his daughter, of course.

She could tell herself that it was a temporary position, that she was only committing two months of her time. But two months was a heck of a long time to maintain her objectivity with respect to a man she'd fallen head over heels for when she was only twelve years old, and a little girl who had taken hold of her heart the very first time she'd met her.

Hannah cranked up the radio in the hope that the pulsing music would push the thoughts out of her head. It didn't.

She wrapped her fingers around the steering wheel, her palms sliding over the smooth leather, and was reminded of the feel of his hand against hers. Warm. Strong. Solid.

She really was pathetic.

She really should have said no when her uncle first suggested that she could be anyone's nanny. But as she drove through the gates toward the prince's summer home, after showing her identification to the guard on duty, she knew that she'd passed the point of no return.

Cielo del Norte was even more impressive than the prince's home in Verde Colinas. Of course, it had once been the royal family's official summer residence, bequeathed to the princess royal by her father upon the occasion of her marriage to Gaetan Leandres.

Hannah had been advised that there were two full-time employees who lived in a guest cottage on the property, the groundskeeper and his wife. Hannah had been thrilled to hear that Caridad, the housekeeper, also cooked and served the meals, because she knew that if she'd been put in charge of food preparation as well as child care, they might all starve before the end of the summer.

She parked her aging little car beside a gleaming black Mercedes SUV and made her way to the door. An older woman in a neatly pressed uniform responded to the bell.

"Mrs. Fuentes?"

"Sí. Caridad Fuentes." She bowed formally. "You are Miss Castillo?"

"Hannah," she said, stepping into the foyer.

"The prince has been expecting you." There was the slightest hint of disapproval beneath the words.

"I was a little late getting away this morning," she explained. "And then traffic was heavier than I expected. Of course, taking a wrong turn at Highway Six didn't help, either, but at least I didn't travel too far out of my way."

The housekeeper didn't comment in any way except to ask, "Are your bags in the car?"

"Yes, I'll get them later."

"Estavan—my husband—will bring them in for you," Mrs. Fuentes told her.

"Okay. That would be great. Thanks." She paused, just taking a minute to absorb the scene.

She'd thought passing through the gates at Verde Colinas had been a culture shock, but now she felt even more like a country mouse set loose in the big city. The house, probably three times the size of the prince's primary residence in Port Augustine, almost seemed as big as a city—a very prosperous and exquisite one.

"There's a powder room down the hall, if you would like to freshen up before meeting with Prince Michael," the housekeeper told her.

Hannah nodded. "I would."

"First door on the right."

"And the prince's office?"

"The third door on the left down the west corridor."

Michael sensed her presence even before he saw her standing in the open doorway. When he looked up, he noticed that she'd dressed less formally today than at their first meeting, and that the jeans and T-shirt she wore made her look even younger than he'd originally guessed. He'd told her that casual attire was acceptable, and there was nothing inappropriate about what she was wearing. But he couldn't help noticing how the denim hugged her thighs and molded to her slim hips. The V-neck of her T-shirt wasn't low enough to give even a glimpse of cleavage, but the soft cotton clung to undeniably feminine curves. She wore silver hoops in her ears, and her hair was in a loose ponytail rather than a tight knot, making her look more approachable and even more beautiful, and he felt the distinct hum of sexual attraction through his veins.

Uncomfortable with the stirring of feelings so long dormant, his voice was a little harsher than he'd intended when he said, "You're late."

Still, his tone didn't seem to faze her. "I told you that I would come as soon as possible, and I did."

"I had a conference call at 8:00 a.m. this morning that I had to reschedule because you weren't here."

He expected that she would apologize or show some sign of remorse. Instead she surprised him by asking, "Why on earth would you schedule a conference call so early on the first morning of your vacation?"

"I told you that I would be conducting business from here," he reminded her. "And your job is to take care of my daughter so that I can focus on doing so."

"A job I'm looking forward to," she assured him.

"I appreciate your enthusiasm," he said. "I would expect that someone who spends ten months out of the year with kids would want a break."

"Spending the summer with a four-year-old is a welcome break from senior advanced English and history," she told him.

Senior English and history? The implications of her statement left him momentarily speechless. "You're a *high school* teacher?" he finally said.

Now it was her turn to frown. "I thought you knew that."

He shook his head. "Phillip said you would be perfect for

the job because you were a teacher—I assumed he meant elementary school."

"Well, you assumed wrong." She shrugged, the casual gesture drawing his attention to the rise and fall of her breasts beneath her T-shirt and very nearly making him forget the reason for his concern.

"So what kind of experience do you have with preschool children, Miss Castillo?" he asked, forcing his gaze back to her face.

"Other than the fact that I was one?" she asked lightly.

"Other than that," he agreed.

"None," she admitted.

"None?" Dios! How could this have happened? He was the consummate planner. He scheduled appointment reminders in his BlackBerry; he took detailed notes at every meeting; he checked and double-checked all correspondence before he signed anything. And yet he'd somehow managed to hire a nanny who knew absolutely nothing about being a nanny.

"Well, my friend Karen has a couple of kids, and I've spent a lot of time with them," Hannah continued.

He shook his head, trying to find solace in the fact that their agreement was for only two months, but he was beginning to question why he'd been in such a hurry to replace Brigitte. Had he been thinking of Riley—or had he been more concerned about maintaining the status quo in his own life? Or maybe he'd been spellbound by Miss Castillo's sparkling eyes and warm smile. Regardless of his reasons, he knew it wasn't her fault that he'd hired her on the basis of some mistaken assumptions. But if she was going to spend the summer with Riley, she had a lot to learn—and fast.

"You'll need this," he said, passing a sheaf of papers across the desk.

In the transfer of the pages, her fingers brushed against his. It was a brief and incidental contact, but he felt the jolt sizzle in his veins. Her gaze shot to meet his, and the widening of her eyes confirmed that she'd felt it, too. That undeniable tug of a distinctly sexual attraction.

As he looked into her eyes, he realized he'd made another mistake in thinking that they were blue—they were actually more gray than blue, the color of the sky before a storm, and just as mesmerizing.

Then she glanced away, down at the papers he'd given to her, and he wondered if maybe he'd imagined both her reaction and his own.

"What is this?" she asked him.

"It's Riley's schedule."

She looked back at him, then at the papers again. "You're kidding."

"A child needs consistency," he said firmly, because it was something Brigitte had always insisted upon, and he usually deferred to the nanny with respect to decisions about his daughter's care.

"If you're referring to a prescribed bedtime, I would absolutely agree," Hannah said. "But a child also needs a chance to be spontaneous and creative, and this—" she glanced at the chart again, obviously appalled "—this even schedules her bathroom breaks."

Maybe the charts Brigitte had prepared for the new nanny did provide a little too much detail, but he understood that she'd only wanted to ease the transition for both Riley and her temporary caregiver. "Brigitte found that taking Riley to the bathroom at prescribed times greatly simplified the toilet-training process."

"But she's almost four years old now," Hannah noted. "I'm sure…" Her words trailed off, her cheeks flushed. "I'm sorry—I just didn't expect that there would be so much to occupy her time."

He'd had some concerns initially, too, but Brigitte had made him see the benefits for Riley. Maybe she was young, but she was so mature for her age, so focused, and she was learning so much. She had a natural musical talent, an artistic touch and a gift for languages, and there was no way he was going to let this temporary nanny upset the status quo with questions and criticisms on her first day on the job. Even if her doubts echoed his own.

"It is now almost eleven o'clock, Miss Castillo," he pointed out to her.

She glanced at the page in her hand. "I guess that means it's almost time for the princess's piano lesson."

"The music room is at the end of the hall."

She folded the schedule and dropped a curtsy.

He deliberately refocused his attention back on the papers on his desk so that he wouldn't watch her walk away.

But he couldn't deny that she tempted him in more ways than he was ready to acknowledge.

Chapter Three

Well, that hadn't gone quite as she'd expected, Hannah thought as she exited Prince Michael's office. And she couldn't help but feel a little disappointed, not just with their meeting but in the man himself. She'd thought he might want to talk to her about Riley's favorite activities at the beach, give her some suggestions on how to keep the little girl busy and happy, but she'd gotten the impression he only wanted her to keep the child occupied and out of his way.

As she made her way down the hall in search of the princess, she realized that she'd never actually seen him with his daughter. The first time she'd met Riley—the day of the ice cream mishap at the art gallery—the little girl had been in the care of her nanny. When Hannah had arrived at the prince's house to interview for the position, Riley had been out with Brigitte. She'd gone back for a second visit, to spend some time with the child so that she wouldn't be a complete stranger to her when she showed up at Cielo del Norte, but she hadn't seen the prince at all on that occasion.

Now he was in his office, and the princess was apparently somewhere else in this labyrinth of rooms preparing for a piano lesson. Did they always lead such separate lives? Did the prince really intend to spend most of his supposed holiday at his desk?

Once she'd gotten over her wariness about taking a job for which she had no experience, she'd actually found herself looking forward to spending the summer with the young princess. She'd imagined that they would play in the water and have picnics on the beach. She hadn't anticipated that the little girl wouldn't have time for fun and frivolity. Yes, she'd been born royal and would someday have duties and obligations as a result, but she wasn't even four years old yet.

Brigitte had made a point of telling Hannah—several times—that Riley was an exceptionally bright and gifted child who was already reading at a second-grade level—in French. She'd encouraged the young princess to demonstrate her talents at the piano, and Riley had done so willingly enough. Hannah couldn't help but be impressed, but in the back of her mind, she wondered why the child didn't seem happy.

Somehow that question had Hannah thinking about what she'd been doing as a four-year-old. Her own childhood had hardly been traditional, but it had been fun. In whatever village had been their current home, she'd always had lots of local children to play with. She'd raced over the hills and played hide-and-seek in the trees. She'd gone swimming in watering holes and rivers and streams. She'd created rudimentary sculptures out of riverbank clay and built houses and castles from mud and grass.

Her parents had never worried about the lack of formal education, insisting that the life skills she was learning were far more important than reading and writing. While the teacher in her cringed at that philosophy now, she did understand the importance of balance between life and learning.

At the princess's age, she'd picked up some words and phrases in Swahili and Hausa and Manyika, enough to communicate with the other kids on a basic level; Riley was studying French, Italian and German out of textbooks. And whereas Hannah had learned music by banging on tribal drums or shaking and rattling dried seed pods, Riley had lessons from professional instructors.

She could hear the piano now, and followed the sound of the sharp, crisp notes to the music room to find the prince's daughter practicing scales on a glossy white Steinway.

She was sitting in the middle of the piano bench, her feet—clad in ruffled ankle socks and white patent Mary Janes—dangling several inches above the polished marble floor. Her long, dark hair was neatly plaited and tied with a pink bow. Her dress was the same shade of cotton candy, with ruffles at the bottoms of the sleeves and skirt. The housekeeper was in the corner, dusting some knickknacks on a shelf and surreptitiously keeping an eye on the princess.

The soaring ceiling was set off with an enormous chandelier dripping with crystals, but the light was unnecessary as the late-morning sun spilled through the tall, arched windows that faced the ocean. The other walls were hung with gorgeous woven tapestries, and while Hannah guessed that their placement was more likely for acoustics than aesthetics, the effect was no less breathtaking.

Suddenly, the fingers moving so smoothly over the ivory keys stopped abruptly. Riley swiveled on the bench, a dark scowl on her pretty face. "What are you doing in here?"

"Hello, Riley," Hannah said pleasantly.

"What are you doing in here?" the princess asked again.

"I wanted to hear you practice."

"I like to be alone when I practice," she said, demonstrating that she'd inherited her father's mood as well as his dark eyes.

Hannah just shrugged, refusing to let the little girl's attitude affect her own. "I can wait in the hall until you're finished."

"I have my French lesson after piano."

Hannah referred to the schedule she'd been given, which confirmed Riley's statement. "I'll see you at lunch, then."

The princess's nod dismissed her as definitively as the prince had done only a few minutes earlier.

On her way out, Hannah passed the piano teacher coming in.

The older woman had a leather bag over her shoulder and determination in her step. Clearly *she* had a purpose for being here. Hannah had yet to figure out her own.

The conference call that Michael had rescheduled came through at precisely eleven o'clock and concluded twenty minutes later. A long time after that, he was still struggling to accept what he'd learned about Miss Castillo—high school teacher turned temporary nanny.

Phillip Marotta had said only that she was a teacher; Michael had assumed that meant she had experience with children. Because he trusted the royal physician implicitly, he had taken the doctor's recommendation without question. Apparently he should have asked some questions, but he acknowledged that the mistake had been his own.

Still, despite the new nanny's apparent lack of experience, he knew that the doctor had stronger reasons than nepotism for suggesting his niece for the job. And from what Brigitte had told him, Riley seemed to accept her easily enough. Of course, his daughter had had so many doctors and teachers and instructors in and out of her life that she accepted most newcomers without any difficulty.

So why was he uneasy about Miss Castillo's presence at

Cielo del Norte? Was he really concerned about Riley—or himself?

When Sam died, he'd thought he would never stop grieving the loss. He was certain he would never stop missing her. But over the years, the pain had gradually started to fade, and Riley's easy affection had begun to fill the emptiness in his heart. He'd been grateful for that, and confident that the love of his little girl was enough.

He didn't need romance or companionship—or so he'd believed until Hannah walked into his life. But he couldn't deny that the new nanny affected him in a way that no woman had done in a very long time.

A brisk knock at the door gave him a reprieve from these melancholy thoughts.

"Lunch will be served on the terrace as soon as you're ready," Caridad told him.

He nodded his thanks as he checked his watch, surprised that so much time had passed. Twenty minutes on the phone followed by an hour and a half of futile introspection. Maybe he did need a vacation.

The housekeeper dropped a quick curtsy before she turned back toward the door.

"Caridad—"

"Yes, Your Highness?"

"What is your impression of Miss Castillo?"

Her eyes widened. "I'm not sure I understand why you'd be asking that, sir."

"Because I value your opinion," he told her honestly. "During the summers that I spent here as a kid, you were always a lot more of a mother to me than my own mother was—which makes you Riley's honorary grandmother and, as such, I'd expect you to have an opinion of her new nanny."

"We've only spoken briefly, sir, I'm certainly not in any position—"

"Quick first impressions," he suggested.

"Well, she's not quite what I expected," Caridad finally admitted.

"In what way?"

"She's very young and...quite attractive."

He didn't think Hannah was as young as Brigitte's twenty-four years, though he could see why the housekeeper might have thought so. Brigitte had dressed more conservatively and she hadn't been nearly as outspoken as the doctor's niece.

"Not that Brigitte wasn't attractive," she clarified. "But she was more...subtle."

She was right. There was absolutely nothing subtle about Hannah Castillo. While she certainly didn't play up her natural attributes, there was something about her—an energy or an aura—that made it impossible for her to fade into the background.

"But I'm sure that neither her age nor her appearance has any relevance to her ability to do her job," she hastened to add.

No—the most relevant factor was her employment history, which he decided not to mention to the housekeeper. No doubt Caridad would wonder how he'd ended up hiring someone with a complete lack of experience, and he was still trying to figure that one out himself.

"If I may speak freely..." Caridad ventured.

"Of course," he assured her.

"You should spend more time around young and beautiful women and less behind your desk."

"Like the young and beautiful woman you 'hired' to help in the kitchen when you sprained your wrist last summer?" he guessed.

"I wasn't sure you'd even noticed," she admitted.

"How could I not when every time I turned around she was in my way?" he grumbled good-naturedly.

"Maybe she was a little obvious, but I thought if I had to

hire someone, it wouldn't hurt to hire someone who might catch your eye."

"Caridad," he said warningly.

"Your daughter needs more than a nanny—she needs a mother."

The quick stab that went through his heart whenever anyone made reference to Samantha's passing—even a reference as veiled as Caridad's—was no longer a surprise, and no longer quite so painful.

"And in a perfect world, she would still have her mother and I would still have my wife," he stated matter-of-factly. "Unfortunately, this is not a perfect world."

"Four years is a long time to grieve," she said in a gentler tone.

"When Sam and I got married, I promised to love her forever. Is that time frame supposed to change just because she's gone?"

"Unless your vows were different than mine, they didn't require you to remain faithful forever but only 'till death do us part.'"

"Could you ever imagine loving anyone other than Estavan?" he countered.

"No," she admitted softly. "But we have been together forty-one years and I am an old woman now. You are still young—you have many years to live and much love to give."

He glanced at the calendar on his desk. "I also have another quick call to make before lunch."

"Of course, Your Highness." She curtsied again, but paused at the door. "I just have one more thing to say."

He knew it was his own fault. Once he'd opened the door, he had no right to stop her from walking through. "What is it?"

"No one questions how much you loved your wife," she told him. "Just as no one would raise an eyebrow now if you decided it was time to stop grieving and start living again."

He hadn't been with anyone since Sam had died, almost four years ago. And he hadn't been with anyone but Sam for the fourteen years before that. He'd loved his wife for most of his life. After meeting her, he'd never wanted anyone else—he'd never even looked twice at any other woman.

But Caridad was right—Hannah Castillo was beautiful, and he'd found himself looking at her and seeing not just his daughter's new nanny but a desirable woman.

Thankfully the buzz of his BlackBerry prevented him from having to respond to the housekeeper. Acknowledging the signal with a nod, she slipped out of the room, closing the door behind her.

Michael picked up the phone, forcing all thoughts of Hannah from his mind.

Lunch for the adults was pan-seared red snapper served with couscous and steamed vegetables. For Riley, it was chicken nuggets and fries with a few vegetables on the side. She eagerly ate the nuggets, alternately played with or nibbled on the fries and carefully rearranged the vegetables on her plate.

Throughout the meal, Hannah was conscious—almost painfully so—of the prince seated across the table. She'd pretty much decided that she didn't really like him, at least not what she'd seen of him so far, but for some inexplicable reason, that didn't stop her pulse from racing whenever he was near. Remnants of her childhood crush? Or the shallow desires of a long-celibate woman? Whatever the explanation, the man sure did interfere with her equilibrium.

Thankfully, he paid little attention to her, seeming content to make conversation with his daughter. Hannah found it interesting to observe their interaction, noting how alive and animated the princess was with her father. Certainly there was no evidence of the moody child who had banished her from the music room earlier.

"Is there something wrong with your fish?"

Hannah was so caught up in her introspection that it took her a moment to realize that the prince had actually deigned to speak to her. She looked down at her plate now, startled to notice that her meal had barely been touched.

"Oh. No." She picked up her fork, speared a chunk of red snapper. "It's wonderful."

"Are you not hungry?"

She *was* hungry. The muffin and coffee that had been her breakfast en route were little more than a distant memory, and the meal the housekeeper had prepared was scrumptious. But not nearly as scrumptious as the man seated across from her—

She felt her cheeks flush in response to the errant thought. "I'm a little nervous," she finally admitted.

"About seafood?"

The teasing note in his voice surprised her, and the corners of her mouth automatically tilted in response to his question. "No. About being here…with you."

"With me," he echoed, his brows drawing together. "Why?"

"Because you're a prince," she admitted. "And I'm not accustomed to dining with royalty."

"I'm a princess," Riley interjected, lest anyone forget her presence at the table.

"It's only a title," her father told both of them.

"That's easy to say when you're the one with the title," Hannah noted.

"Maybe," he agreed. "But the matter of anyone's birthright seems a strange reason to miss out on a delicious meal."

She scooped up a forkful of vegetables, dutifully slid it between her lips. "You're right—and it is delicious."

She managed to eat a few more bites before she noticed the princess was yawning. "Someone looks like she's ready for a nap," she noted.

"I don't nap," Riley informed her primly. "I have quiet time."

"Right, I saw that on the schedule," Hannah recalled, noting that Brigitte had indicated "nap" in parentheses.

And then, as if on schedule, the little girl yawned again.

"I think you're ready for that quiet time," the prince said, glancing at his watch.

His daughter shook her head. "I want ice cream."

He hesitated.

"Please, Daddy." She looked up at him with her big brown eyes.

"Actually, Caridad said something about crème caramel for dessert tonight," he said, attempting to put off her request.

"I want ice cream now," Riley insisted.

"One scoop or two?" Caridad asked, clearing the luncheon plates from the table.

"Two," the princess said enthusiastically. "With chocolate sauce and cherries."

The housekeeper brought out the little girl's dessert, but as eagerly as the child dug in to her sundae, Hannah didn't believe she would finish it. Sure enough, Riley's enthusiasm began to wane about halfway through, but she surprised Hannah by continuing to move her spoon from the bowl to her mouth until it was all gone.

"Could I please have some more?" Riley asked when Caridad came back out to the terrace, looking up at the housekeeper with the same big eyes and sweet smile that she'd used so effectively on her father.

"You can have more after dinner," the housekeeper promised.

The upward curve of Riley's lips immediately turned down. "But I'm still hungry."

"If you were really still hungry, you should have asked

for some more chicken, not more ice cream," the prince told his daughter.

"I didn't want more chicken," she said with infallible logic.

Hannah pushed away from the table. "Come on, Riley. Let's go get you washed up."

"I'm not a baby—I don't need help washing up."

It seemed to Hannah that the young princess didn't need help with much of anything—certainly not with manipulating the adults in her life, a talent which she had definitely mastered.

But she kept that thought to herself, at least for now.

She didn't want to lose her job on the first day.

"Riley," Michael chastised, embarrassed by his daughter's belligerent response. "Hannah is only trying to help."

"Actually," Hannah interjected, speaking to Riley, "maybe you could help me."

The little girl's eyes narrowed suspiciously. "With what?"

"Finding my way around this place," the new nanny said. "I've only been here a few hours and I've gotten lost three times already. Maybe you could show me where you spend your quiet time."

Riley pushed away from the table, dramatically rolling her eyes as she did so. If Hannah noticed his daughter's theatrics, she chose to ignore them.

"If you'll excuse us, Your Highness," she said.

"Of course." He rose with her, and watched as she followed Riley into the house.

He wasn't pleased by his daughter's behavior, but he didn't know what to do about it. As much as he loved Riley, he wasn't blind to her faults. But the adolescent attitude in the preschooler's body was just one more of the challenges of parenting a gifted child, or so he'd been told. Was Riley's behavior atypical—or did he just not know what was typical for a child of her age?

Surely any four-year-old going through a period of adjustment would need some time, and losing her longtime nanny was definitely an adjustment. He hoped that within a few days, after Riley had a chance to get to know Hannah and settle into new routines with her, her usual sunny disposition would return.

After all, it was a new situation for all of them, and it was only day one.

But as he made his way back to his office, he found himself thinking that he probably missed Brigitte even more than his daughter did. Everything had run smoothly when Brigitte was around.

More importantly, he'd never felt any tugs of attraction for the former nanny like the ones he was feeling now for Hannah.

Chapter Four

According to Brigitte's schedule, Riley's quiet time was from two o'clock until three-thirty. When that time came and went, Hannah didn't worry. She figured the little girl wouldn't still be sleeping if she wasn't tired, and since there wasn't anything else on her schedule until an art class at four-thirty, she opted not to disturb her before then.

Hannah was staring at her laptop screen when she heard, through the open door across the hallway, what sounded like drawers being pulled open and shut. She immediately closed the lid on her computer, wishing she could as easily shut down the shock and betrayal evoked by her father's email announcement.

He'd gotten married, without ever telling her of his plans, without even letting her meet the woman who was now his wife. But she forced herself to push those emotions aside and crossed the hall to the princess's room, a ready smile on her lips, determined to start the afternoon with Riley on a better foot.

Riley didn't smile back. Instead, she scowled again and her lower lip trembled.

"I want Brigitte," she demanded.

"You know Brigitte isn't here," Hannah said, attempting to keep her tone gentle and soothing.

"I want Brigitte," Riley said again.

"Maybe I can help with whatever you need," she suggested.

The young princess shook her head mutinously, big tears welling in her eyes. "It's your fault."

"What's my fault?"

"You made me wet the bed."

Only then did Hannah notice that the little girl wasn't wearing the same dress she'd had on when she'd settled on her bed for quiet time. She was wearing a short-sleeved white blouse with a blue chiffon skirt now, and the lovely pink dress was in a heap on the floor beside her dresser. A quick glance at the unmade bed revealed a damp circle.

"Accidents happen," Hannah said lightly, pulling back the covers to strip away the wet sheet. "It will only—"

"It wasn't an accident," Riley insisted. "It was your fault."

Hannah knew the child was probably upset and embarrassed and looking to blame anyone else, but she couldn't help asking, "How, exactly, is it my fault?"

"You're supposed to get me up at three-thirty—when the big hand is on the six and the little hand is halfway between the three and the four," Riley explained. "But now it's after four o'clock."

She probably shouldn't have been surprised that the child knew how to tell time—that basic skill was hardly on par with speaking foreign languages—and she began to suspect that the next two months with Riley would be more of a challenge than she'd imagined.

"Brigitte would have woke me up," Riley said, swiping at the tears that spilled onto her cheeks.

"*Woken*," Hannah corrected automatically as she dropped the sheet into the hamper beside Riley's closet. "And I know you miss Brigitte a lot, but hopefully we can be friends while I'm here."

"You're not my friend, you're the new nanny, and I hate you."

"I promise that you and I will have lots of fun together this summer. We can go—"

"I don't want to go anywhere with you. I just want *you* to go *away!*" Riley demanded with such fierce insistence that Hannah felt her own eyes fill with tears.

She knew that she shouldn't take the little girl's rejection personally. Despite her extensive vocabulary and adolescent attitude, Riley was only a child, reacting to her feelings of loss and abandonment. But Hannah understood those feelings well—maybe too well, with the news of her father's recent marriage still fresh in her mind—and she hated that she couldn't take away her pain.

"What's going on in here?" a familiar, masculine voice asked from the doorway.

Riley flew across the room and into her father's arms, sobbing as if the whole world had fallen down around her.

The prince lifted her easily. "What's with the tears?"

"I want Brigitte to come back." She wrapped her arms around his neck and buried her face against his throat, crying softly.

He frowned at Hannah over her daughter's head, as if the new nanny was somehow responsible for the child's tears.

"She's feeling abandoned," she told him.

His brows lifted. "Is she?"

She couldn't help but bristle at the obvious amusement in his tone. Maybe she didn't know his daughter very well yet, but she understood at least some of what the little girl was feeling, and she wasn't going to let him disregard the depth of those feelings.

"Yes, she is," she insisted. "She was upset when she woke up and the only person who was anywhere around was me—a virtual stranger."

The prince rubbed his daughter's back in an easy way that suggested he'd done so countless times before. "She'll get used to being here and to being with you," he insisted.

Hannah wished she could believe it was true, but she sensed that the princess would resist at every turn. "Maybe, eventually," she allowed. "But in the meantime, you're the only constant in her life and you weren't around."

"I was only downstairs," he pointed out.

"Behind closed doors."

"If I didn't have other things to deal with, Miss Castillo, I wouldn't have hired you to help take care of Riley for the summer." Now that the little girl had quieted, he set her back on her feet.

Hannah wanted to ask if his business was more important than his daughter, but she knew that it wasn't a fair question. She had to remember that the prince wasn't her own father, and she couldn't assume that his preoccupation with other matters meant he didn't care about the princess.

"You're right," she agreed, watching as Riley went over to her desk to retrieve a portfolio case. "I'm sorry. I just wish this wasn't so difficult for her."

"I get the impression she's making it difficult for you, too."

She hadn't expected he would see that, much less acknowledge it, and she conceded that she may have been a little too quick to judgment.

"I teach *Beowulf* to football players—I don't mind a challenge," she said lightly. "Although right now, the challenge seems to be finding a spare set of sheets for Riley's bed."

"I'll send Caridad up to take care of it," he told her.

"I don't mind," she said, thinking that it would at least

be something useful for her to do. "I just need you to point me in the direction of the linen closet."

Before he could respond, Riley interjected, "I need flowers for my art project."

"Why don't you go outside with Hannah to get some from the gardens?" the prince suggested. "I'm sure she would love to see the flowers."

"Can't you come with me, Daddy?" she asked imploringly.

"I'm sorry, honey, but I have a big project to finish up before dinner."

With a sigh, Riley finally glanced over at Hannah, acknowledging her for the first time since the prince had come into the room.

"I need freesias," she said. "Do you know what they are?"

Hannah smiled. "As a matter of fact, freesias happen to be some of my favorite flowers."

Michael was going to his office to pick up a file when the phone on the desk rang. He'd just tucked Riley into bed and didn't want her to wake up, so he answered quickly, without first bothering to check the display. The moment he heard his mother's voice, he realized his mistake.

"I have wonderful news for you, Michael."

"What news is that?" he asked warily, having learned long ago that her idea of wonderful didn't always jibe with his own.

"Your daughter has been accepted for admission at Charlemagne Académie."

"I didn't even know she'd applied," he said dryly.

Elena huffed out an impatient breath. "I pulled a lot of strings to make this happen, Michael. A little appreciation would not be unwarranted."

"I didn't ask you to pull any strings," he pointed out. "In fact, I'm certain I never mentioned Charlemagne at all."

"Your sister went there—it's a wonderful educational institution."

"Even so, I'm not sending Riley to boarding school."

"Of course you are," Elena insisted. "And while they don't usually accept children as young as five—"

"Riley's not yet four," he interrupted.

His mother paused, as if taken aback by this revelation, but she recovered quickly. "Well, if they could take a five-year-old, they can take a four-year-old."

"They're not taking her at all," he said firmly.

"Be reasonable, Michael. This is the perfect solution to your child-care dilemma."

"There's no dilemma, no reason for you to worry."

"I thought your nanny was leaving."

"Brigitte did leave, and I hired someone new for the summer."

"And what will you do at the end of the summer?" she challenged.

"I'm not worrying about that right now."

"The fall term starts in September."

"I'm not sending my four-year-old daughter away to boarding school in Switzerland."

"The child will benefit from the structure and discipline."

"The child has a name," he pointed out.

"A wholly inappropriate one for a princess," his mother sniffed.

"You've made your opinion on that perfectly clear," he assured her. "But it doesn't change the fact that Riley is her name."

"Getting back to my point—*Riley* will benefit from the structure and discipline at Charlemagne, and you will no longer be burdened—"

"Don't." Though softly spoken, the single word silenced her as effectively as a shout. "Don't you dare even suggest that my daughter is a burden."

"I didn't mean that the chi—that *Riley* was a burden," she hastened to explain. "But that the responsibilities of caring for a young daughter must seem overwhelming at times."

He couldn't deny that was true any more than he could expect his mother to understand that Riley was also the greatest joy in his life, so he only said, "I'll let you know if I change my mind about Charlemagne."

"I really do believe it would be best for Riley and for you," she said.

"I appreciate your concern," he lied.

Elena sighed. "I'll look forward to hearing from you."

Michael began to respond, but she'd already disconnected the call.

He dropped the receiver back in the cradle and went around his desk. Only then did he notice the figure curled up in the oversized wing chair facing the fireplace.

"I beg your pardon, Your Highness." Hannah immediately rose to her feet. "I should have made my presence known, but I didn't have a chance to say anything before the phone rang. Then I wanted to leave and to give you some privacy for your call, but you were blocking the door."

He waved off her apology. "It's okay."

"I really didn't intend to eavesdrop," she assured him. "But for what it's worth, I'm glad you're not planning to send Riley to boarding school."

He shook his head. "I can't believe she would expect me to even consider such a thing."

"She?" Hannah prompted curiously.

"My mother."

Her eyes widened. "That was your mother on the phone?"

He could only imagine how his half of the conversation had sounded to her, and shrugged. "We don't have a traditional parent-child relationship," he said.

Truthfully, there was more apathy than affection between them, especially since his wife had died. Elena had never respected boundaries and had never trusted her children to make their own decisions, and he had yet to forgive her for interfering in his marriage and convincing Sam that it was her wifely duty to provide him with an heir—a decision that had ultimately cost her life.

"Riley's grandmother wanted to send her to Switzerland?" Hannah pressed, apparently unable to get past that point.

"She even pulled strings to ensure she would be accommodated," he said.

"But she's just a child."

"My mother isn't an advocate of hands-on parenting," Michael told her.

Hannah seemed to think about this for a minute, then asked, "Did you go to boarding school?"

He nodded. "My brother and sister and I all did, but not until high school. Before that, we attended Wyldewood Collegiate."

"It would be easy to send her away," she said. "To let someone else assume the day-to-day responsibilities of her care."

"No, it wouldn't," he denied. "It would be the hardest thing in the world."

Hannah's conversation with the prince gave her some unexpected insight into his character and a lot to think about, but she was mostly preoccupied with trying to figure out his daughter. She tried to be patient and understanding, but as one day turned into two and then three, it seemed that nothing she said or did could change the princess's attitude toward her. And if there was one thing Hannah was certain of, it was that the princess's attitude very definitely needed changing.

On Saturday, after Riley had finished her lessons for the day, Hannah decided to take the little girl down to the beach. She'd made a trip into town the day before to get buckets and shovels and various other sand toys, and she was excited to watch Riley play. She should have guessed that the child would be less than enthusiastic about her plans.

"I don't like sand," the princess informed her. "And I get hot in the sun."

"That's why we wear our bathing suits—so we can cool off in the ocean after we play in the sand."

Riley folded her arms over her chest. "You can't make me go."

"Go where?" the prince asked, stepping out of his office in time to catch the tail end of their conversation.

"Hannah's trying to make me go to the beach." She made it sound as if her nanny was proposing a new kind of water torture.

"That sounds like a lot of fun."

The little girl wrinkled her nose, clearly unconvinced. "Will you come with us?"

He hesitated, and Hannah knew he was going to refuse, so she spoke quickly, responding before he did in the hope that it might lessen the sting of his refusal for Riley.

"I'm sure your daddy would love to come if he didn't have important business that needed his attention right now."

"But it's Saturday," Riley said, looking up at him pleadingly.

"Well, in that case," he said, "I could probably play hooky for a couple of hours."

His daughter's eyes lit up. "Really?"

"Sure, just give me a few minutes to change."

While the prince disappeared to don more appropriate beach attire, Hannah made sure that the princess was covered in sunscreen. Although the little girl obviously didn't like having the cream rubbed on her skin, she didn't protest. Apparently she was willing to put up with the process—and even Hannah—so long as she got to go to the beach with her daddy.

Hannah glanced up when she heard his footsteps, and exhaled a quiet sigh of purely female admiration. Over the past week, she'd come to appreciate how good the prince looked in his customary Armani trousers and Turnbull & Asser shirts, but the more formal attire had given her no indication of how muscular and toned he was beneath the clothes. Now he was wearing only board shorts slung low on his hips with a striped beach towel draped across very strong, broad shoulders, and just looking at him made Hannah's knees go weak.

She'd admired him from afar for so many years. As a teen, she'd snipped every photo of him out of newspapers and magazines and created her own personal scrapbook. Back then, she'd never expected that their paths would ever cross again. And now he was only a few feet away from her—almost close enough to touch. In fact, if she took only two steps forward, she could lay her hands on his smooth, tanned chest to feel the warmth of his skin and the beating of his heart beneath her palms. She could—

"Are we ready?" he asked.

"I'm ready, Daddy!"

It was the excitement in the little girl's response that snapped Hannah out of her fantasy and back to the present. She reached down for the bucket of toys, conscious of the warm flush in her cheeks. She should have outgrown her adolescent crush on the prince long ago, but as embarrassing as it was to accept that some of those feelings remained, it was somehow worse to realize that the man she was ogling was her boss. Obviously she had to work on maintaining appropriate boundaries.

"Let's go," she said brightly.

She'd barely taken a dozen steps out the door when she heard a familiar chime. Startled, she turned back to see the prince reaching into the pocket of his shorts.

"You weren't really planning to take your BlackBerry down to the beach, were you?" she asked incredulously.

"I've been waiting to hear back from a new client," he said without apology. And without another word, he turned away and connected the call.

Riley watched him, her big brown eyes filled with disappointment.

Hannah shook her head, acknowledging that while the prince might have a fabulous body and a face worthy of magazine covers, his priorities were completely screwed up.

Then she remembered the telephone conversation she'd overheard and the prince's adamant refusal to send his daughter away to school. Obviously he loved his little girl and wanted to keep her close—so why did he keep himself so distant from her? And why was she so determined to uncover the reason for this contradictory behavior?

Pushing the question from her mind, at least for now, she continued toward the water and the expensive private beach that had been calling to Hannah since her arrival at Cielo del Norte. "Do you want to know one of my favorite things about the beach?" she asked the princess.

The little girl shrugged but trudged along beside her.

"When the waves break against the shore, you can give them your troubles and they'll take them back out to the sea."

"No, they won't," the princess protested.

But instead of her usual confrontational tone, this time the denial was spoken softly, and the quiet resignation in her voice nearly broke Hannah's heart.

"Well, not really," she agreed. "But I'll show you what I mean."

She found a long stick and with it, she wrote in the sand, right at the water's edge: M-A-R-K-I-N-G-T-E-S-T-S.

"I'm a teacher," she explained. "And I love teaching, but I don't like marking tests."

The little girl looked neither interested nor impressed, but she did watch and within a few moments, the movement of the water over the sand had completely erased the letters.

Hannah offered the stick to Riley, to give her a turn. The princess seemed to consider for a moment, then shook her head.

So Hannah wrote again: T-O-F-U. She smiled when the letters washed away.

"What's tofu?" Riley asked.

"Bean curd," Hannah said. "It comes from China and is used in a lot of vegetarian dishes."

Thinking of China made her think of Ian, so she wrote his name in the sand.

"Who's Ian?"

"Someone I thought was a friend, but who turned out not to be. He's in China now."

"Eating tofu?"

She chuckled at Riley's question. "I don't know—maybe he is."

The little princess reached for the stick. She paused with the point of it above the sand, her teeth nibbling on her bottom lip. Finally she began to make letters, carefully focusing on the formation of each one until she spelled out: R-A-M.

"You don't like sheep?"

Riley smiled, just a little. "It's 'Riley Advertising Media.'"

"Your dad's company?"

The little girl nodded.

Hannah frowned as a strange thought suddenly occurred to her. "Did he actually name you after his business?"

Now the princess shook her head. "Riley was my mommy's middle name—because it was her mommy's name before she married my granddad."

"Oh. Well, it makes more sense that you'd be named after your mom than a corporation," Hannah said lightly.

But the little girl was writing in the sand again, this time spelling out: H-A-N-A…

She tried not to take it personally. After all, this game had been her idea, and she should feel grateful that Riley was finally communicating with her, even if she didn't like what she was communicating.

"Actually, my name is spelled like this," she said, and wrote H-A-N-N-A-H in the sand.

Riley studied the word for a moment, and when it washed away, she wrote it again, a little further from the waves this time. "Your name is the same backwards as forwards."

Hannah nodded. "It's called a palindrome."

"Are there other palindromes?"

"There are lots, not just words—" she wrote R-A-C-E-C-A-R in the sand "—but phrases and even complete sentences."

"Do you know any sentences or phrases?" Riley challenged.

N-E-V-E-R-O-D-D-O-R-E-V-E-N.

"That's pretty cool," the princess admitted. Her gaze flickered back toward the house. The prince was pacing on the terrace, his phone still attached to his ear.

She took the stick from Hannah again and wrote D-A-D.

"Good job," Hannah said, then winced when the little girl crossed the word out with so much force the stick snapped.

"Do you want to go back inside?" she asked gently.

Riley shook her head again. "I need to wash off this sand."

Michael had just ended his call when he spotted Hannah and Riley coming out of the water. Obviously he'd missed the opportunity to join them for a swim, and he was as sincerely disappointed as he knew his daughter would be. But as she made her way up the beach with Hannah toward the lounge chairs where they'd left their towels, his attention and his thoughts shifted from his little girl to the woman with her.

He hadn't expected that she would swim in the shorts and T-shirt she'd worn down to the beach. Truthfully, he hadn't even let himself think about what kind of bathing suit she had on beneath those clothes. But it wasn't the bathing suit that snared his attention so much as the delectable curves showcased by the simple one-piece suit of cerulean Lycra.

He didn't feel the phone slip from his fingers until it hit the top of his foot. With a muttered curse, he bent to retrieve the discarded instrument—and smacked his head on the rail coming up again. This time his curse wasn't at all muted.

Rather than risk further bodily injury, he remained where he was, watching through the slats of the railing as the nanny helped Riley dry off. After his daughter's cover-up had been slipped back on, Hannah picked up a second towel and began rubbing it over her own body. From the curve of her shoulders, down slender, shapely arms. From narrow hips, down endlessly long and sleekly muscled legs. Across her collarbone, dipping into the hollow between her breasts.

There was nothing improper about her actions—certainly she wasn't trying to be deliberately seductive. But like a voyeur, he couldn't tear his gaze away.

She tugged her shirt over her head, then shimmied into her shorts, and Michael blew out a long, slow breath, urging the hormones rioting in his system to settle down. But he now knew that, regardless of what she might be wearing, he would forever see the image of her rising out of the water like a goddess.

It was a good thing he would be going out of town for a few days.

Chapter Five

By the time Michael joined his daughter and her new nanny, Riley was packing sand into a long rectangular mold. She glanced up when he lowered himself onto the sand beside her, but didn't say a word. She didn't need to say anything—he could tell by the reproachful look in her big brown eyes that she was displeased with him.

He could handle her quick mood changes and even her temper tantrums, but her evident disappointment cut him to the quick. He was trying his best to be a good father, though it seemed increasingly apparent to him that he didn't know how. Every time he thought he was getting the hang of things, the rules changed.

"Sorry I missed swimming," he said, tugging gently on a lock of her wet hair. "But that was a really important client."

"They're all really important." She turned the mold over and smacked the bottom of it, perhaps a little too hard, with the back of a plastic shovel.

She was right. And she certainly wouldn't be the first person to suggest that he might be too focused on his company. But his work was at least something he understood. In his office, he was competent and capable and completely in charge. With Riley, he often felt helpless and overwhelmed and absolutely terrified that he was going to screw up—as if he hadn't done so enough already.

He glanced over at the nanny, to gauge her interpretation of the stilted exchange with his daughter, but Hannah's eyes were hidden behind dark glasses so that he couldn't tell what she was thinking. He decided he would wait to tell both of them of the meeting that would take him back to the city on Monday.

"What are you making?" he asked Riley instead.

"What does it look like?"

He wasn't pleased by her sarcastic tone, but he knew that she wasn't pleased with him at the moment, either, so he only said, "It looks like a sand castle."

She didn't respond.

"Is it Cinderella's castle or Sleeping Beauty's?" he prompted.

"Uncle Rowan's."

He should have realized that a child who had run through the halls of an authentic castle would be less fascinated by the fairy-tale versions. He should also have realized that she would be as methodical and determined in this task as with any other. Riley didn't like to do anything unless she could do it well. As a result, she quickly grew frustrated with any task she couldn't master.

Though Hannah didn't say anything, she pushed a cylindrical mold toward him with her foot. He let his gaze drift from the tips of her crimson-painted toenails to the slim ankle, along the curve of her slender calf—

She nudged the cylinder again, with a little less patience

this time. He tore his attention away from her shapely legs and picked up the vessel.

"Building a castle is a pretty big project for one person," he said to Riley. "Do you think maybe I could help?"

She just shrugged, so he picked up the small shovel and began filling the receptacle.

"You can't use that sand," she said impatiently, grabbing the mold from him and tipping it upside down to empty it out. "You need the wet stuff, so it sticks together."

She looked to Hannah for verification, confirming that this castle-building knowledge had been recently imparted by the new nanny, and was rewarded by a nod. Then she demonstrated for him—showing him how to pack the container with sand, then turn it over and tap it out again.

There were a few moments of frustration: first when one of the walls collapsed, and again when she realized the windows she'd outlined weren't even. But Michael patiently helped her rebuild the wall and assured her that sand-castle windows wouldn't fall out if they weren't perfectly level. That comment finally elicited a small smile from her, and he basked in the glow of it.

While he remained outwardly focused on the castle-building project, he was conscious of the nanny watching their interactions. He was conscious of the nicely rounded breasts beneath her T-shirt, and of the long, lean legs stretched out on the sand. He noticed that her hair had dried quickly in the sun and that the ends of her ponytail now fluttered in the breeze.

She could have passed for a teenager who'd skipped school to hang out at the beach with her friends, the way she was leaning back on her elbows, her bare feet crossed at the ankles and her face tipped up to the sun. And his immediate physical response to the sexy image was shockingly adolescent.

Dios, it was going to be a long two months. Especially if, as he suspected, he was going to spend an inordinate amount of that time fighting this unexpected attraction to her. On the other hand, the time might pass much more quickly and pleasantly if he *stopped* fighting the attraction. If he reached over right now to unfasten the band that held her hair back in order to slide his hands through the silky mass and tip her head back to taste her—

"Is it okay to dig a moat?" Riley asked, and the fantasy building in his mind dissipated.

He forced his gaze and his attention back to her construction.

"Every castle should have a moat," he assured her.

"Uncle Rowan's doesn't."

"But it should, to protect the princes and princesses inside from ogres and dragons."

She giggled. "Ogres and dragons aren't real, Daddy."

"Maybe not," he allowed. "But a moat is a good idea, just in case."

Riley tipped her head, as if considering, then nodded and began digging.

"What do you think?" he asked Hannah. "Is it worthy of the Sand Castle Hall of Fame?"

"An impressive first effort, Your Highness," she replied, and he knew she wasn't just talking about the construction.

"But I shouldn't quit my day job?" he guessed lightly.

"I don't imagine you would ever consider doing so."

He winced at the direct hit.

"But if you did, you might have a future in castle-building," she relented. "Your spire looks pretty good."

His brows rose. "My spire?"

Her cheeks colored as she gestured to the cone shape on top of the tower he'd built. She was obviously flustered by his innuendo, and he couldn't help but smile at her.

"But your flagpole is crooked," she said, and smiled back at him.

His gaze dropped automatically to her mouth, to the seductive curve of her lips. He wondered if they would feel as soft as they looked, if they would taste as sweet as he imagined. And he thought again about leaning forward to press his mouth to hers, to discover the answers to those questions.

Instead, he straightened the twig that was the castle flag and mused that it had been a long time since he'd shared this kind of light, teasing banter with a woman. A long time since he'd felt the slightest hint of attraction for a woman who wasn't his wife, and what he was feeling for Hannah was more than a hint.

He pushed himself up from the sand and picked up an empty bucket.

"Let's get some water for your moat," he said to Riley.

When the moat was filled and the finished project adequately *ooh*ed and *aah*ed over, they returned to the house. Hannah ran a bath for the princess so that Riley could wash the salt off her body and out of her hair. When she was dried and dressed, the little girl had taken a book and curled up on her bed. Hannah suspected that she would be asleep before she'd finished a single page.

After she'd showered and changed, the nanny ventured back downstairs, looking for Caridad to inquire if the housekeeper needed any help with the preparations for dinner. Hannah was embarrassingly inept in the kitchen but with so much time on her hands, she thought she might start hanging around while Caridad cooked. Even if she didn't learn anything, she enjoyed spending time with the older woman.

Unfortunately, the kitchen was empty when she entered. But more distressing to Hannah than the missing housekeeper was the absence of any suggestion that dinner might be in the oven.

She opened the door and scanned inside, just to be sure. Then she opened the fridge and surveyed the shelves.

"Looking for something?"

She started at the unexpected sound of the prince's voice behind her. When they'd returned to the house, she'd assumed that he would retreat to his office and stay there for the rest of the evening. That was, after all, his pattern.

"Caridad," Hannah said. "I haven't seen her all day."

"Well, I can assure you that you won't find her in either the oven or the refrigerator."

He smiled, to show that he was teasing, and she felt her cheeks flush. She hadn't yet figured out the prince or her feelings for him—aside from the jolt of lust she felt whenever he was in the same room. But as attracted as she was to Prince Michael, she was equally frustrated with the father in him. There were times he was so oblivious to his daughter and her needs that Hannah wanted to throttle him. And then there were other times, such as when he'd reached for his little girl's hand on the beach or when he'd slip into his daughter's room late at night just to watch over her while she slept—as she noticed he did almost every night—that his obvious love and affection for the princess made her heart melt. How could one man be both so distant and so devoted?

And how, she wondered, could one man have her so completely tied up in knots? Because there was no doubt that he did, and Hannah had absolutely no idea how to cope with her feelings.

She tried to ignore them, all too aware that Michael was completely out of her league, not just because he was her boss but because he was a prince. Her short-lived engagement to a British earl had forced her to accept that royals and commoners didn't mix, at least for the long term. Unfortunately, ignoring her feelings for the prince hadn't diminished them in the least.

"She and Estavan have weekends off," Michael continued

his response to her question about Caridad. "Unless I have formal plans for entertaining."

"Oh," Hannah replied inanely, thinking that was another check in the 'good prince' column. She also thought it was great for the housekeeper and her husband—and not so great for a woman whose kitchen expertise was limited to reheating frozen dinners.

"You don't cook, do you?" the prince guessed.

"Not very well," she admitted.

"Then it's a good thing I'm in charge of dinner tonight."

She stared at him. "*You* cook?"

"Why do you sound so surprised?"

"I just can't picture you standing over the stove with a slotted spoon in one hand and your BlackBerry in the other. Your Highness."

Rather than taking offense, he smiled. "You do that a lot, you know."

"What's that?"

"Tack my title on to the end of a reply, as if that might take the sting out of the personal commentary."

"I don't mean to sound disrespectful, Your Highness."

"I'm sure you don't," he drawled. "But getting back to dinner, maybe you could try picturing the stove as a barbecue and the slotted spoon as a set of tongs."

"I should have realized that when you said you could cook what you really meant was that you could grill meat over fire."

"You forgot the 'Your Highness.'"

She smiled sweetly. "Your Highness."

"And at the risk of spoiling your illusions, I will confess that I also make an exquisite alfredo sauce, a delicious stuffed pork loin and a mouthwatering quiche Lorraine."

"But do you actually eat the quiche?" she teased.

"You can answer that question for yourself as it's on the menu for brunch tomorrow."

"And what's on the menu for dinner tonight?" she asked, as curious as she was hungry.

"Steak, baked potato and tossed green salad," he told her.

Her mouth was already watering. "Can I help with anything?"

"You just said that you don't cook."

"Can I help with anything that doesn't involve preparing food over a heat source?" she clarified.

He chuckled. "Do you know how to make a salad?"

"I think I can figure it out."

While Michael cooked potatoes and grilled steaks on the barbecue, Hannah found the necessary ingredients in the refrigerator for a salad. When Riley came downstairs, she gave her the napkins and cutlery and asked her to set them on the table.

The princess did so, though not happily. Obviously she wasn't accustomed to performing any kind of menial chores. And when her father came in with the steaks and potatoes, she looked at the food with obvious distaste.

"Can I have nuggets?"

"Not tonight." The prince had earlier uncorked a bottle of merlot and now poured the wine into two glasses.

"But I want nuggets," Riley said.

"You had nuggets for lunch," Hannah reminded her, and gave herself credit for not adding "almost every day this week."

The little girl folded her arms across her chest. "I want nuggets again."

"If she'd rather have nuggets, I can throw some in the oven," the prince relented.

"Yes, please, Daddy." Riley beamed at him.

Hannah opened her mouth, then closed it again without saying a word.

"Excuse us," he said to his daughter, then caught Hannah's arm and steered her into the kitchen.

"What's the problem with Riley having chicken nuggets?" he demanded.

"I didn't say anything, Your Highness."

"No, you stopped yourself from saying whatever was on your mind," he noted. "And since you didn't seem to have any qualms about speaking up earlier, why are you censoring your comments now?"

"Because I don't want to get fired after less than a week on the job."

"I won't fire you," he promised.

"Then I'll admit that I'm concerned about your willingness to give in to your daughter's demands," she told him. "She's not even four years old, and if you let her dictate what she's going to eat, she might never eat anything but chicken nuggets."

"It's just nuggets."

"No, it's not just nuggets. It's that you always give in to her demands."

"I don't always," he denied.

"And if you give in on all of the little things," she continued, "she'll expect you to give in on the not-so-little things and then, suddenly, you have no authority anymore."

She picked up the salad to carry it to the table, giving the prince a moment to think about what she'd said.

"Where are my nuggets?" Riley demanded when he followed Hannah into the dining room.

"It will take too long to make nuggets now," he said gently. "Why don't you just have what we're having tonight?"

Hannah cut a few pieces of meat from one of the steaks and slid them onto a plate along with half of a baked potato and a scoopful of salad. Although the prince didn't sound as firm as she hoped he would, she gave him credit for at least taking a stand.

The princess scowled at the food when it was set in front of her, then looked straight at Hannah as she picked the plate up and dropped it on the floor.

"Riley!" The prince was obviously shocked by his daughter's behavior.

The little girl, equally shocked by her father's harsh reprimand, burst into tears.

Hannah simply retrieved the broken plate from the floor and scooped up the discarded food to dump it into the garbage. Then she got another plate and prepared it the same way again.

"I want nuggets," Riley said, but her tone was more pleading than demanding now, and tears swam in her big brown eyes.

"Your daddy cooked steak and potatoes. You should at least try that before asking for something else."

Two fat tears tracked slowly down the child's cheeks. "You're mean."

"Because I won't let you have your own way?" Hannah asked.

"Because you told Daddy not to let me have nuggets."

She caught the prince's eye across the table. He looked helpless and confused, and though her heart instinctively went out to him, she felt confident that the situation was of his own making.

"You should sit down and eat your dinner," she suggested quietly.

He sat, but he continued to cast worried glances in his daughter's direction.

"If Riley's hungry, she'll eat," Hannah reassured him.

"I'm hungry for nuggets," the princess insisted.

"You're hungry for power." The retort slipped out before she could clamp her lips together.

Riley frowned at that.

"Don't you think that's a little unfair?" Michael asked.

"No, but I do think your daughter's demands are some-times unreasonable." Hannah finished making up Riley's second plate, but the mutinous look in the little girl's eyes as they zeroed in on the meal warned her that the food was likely destined for the floor again. So instead of setting it in front of her, she put it aside, out of Riley's reach.

Then Hannah deliberately cut into her own steak, slid a tender morsel into her mouth. Riley watched through nar-rowed eyes, her bottom lip quivering. Hannah ate a few more bites of her meal while the child watched, her gaze occasionally shifting to her own plate.

"I'm thirsty," Riley finally announced.

"There's milk in your cup," Hannah told her.

The princess folded her arms across her chest. "I don't want milk."

"Then you can't be very thirsty."

"I want juice," Riley said, and pushed the cup of milk away with such force that it hit Hannah's wineglass, knock-ing the crystal goblet against her plate so that it spilled all over her dinner and splashed down the front of Hannah's shirt.

She gasped and pushed away from the table, but the wine was already trickling down her chest, between her breasts. The prince grabbed his napkin and rounded the table, his gaze focused on the merlot spreading across her top. He squatted beside her chair and began dabbing at the stain.

Hannah went completely still. She couldn't move. She couldn't think. Heck, she couldn't even breathe, because when she tried, she inhaled his distinctly masculine scent and her hormones began to riot in her system. So she sat there, motionless and silent, as he stroked the napkin over the swell of her breasts.

Her blood was pulsing in her veins and her heart was pounding against her ribs, and he was all but oblivious to the effect he was having on her. Or so she thought, until his movements slowed, and his gaze lifted.

His eyes, dark and hot, held hers for a long minute. "I guess I should let you finish that," he said, tucking the linen into her hand.

She only nodded, unable to speak as his gaze dipped again, to where the aching peaks of her nipples pressed against the front of her shirt, as if begging for his attention.

"Or maybe you should change," he suggested, his eyes still riveted on her chest.

She nodded again.

"I want juice!"

Riley's demand broke through the tension that had woven around them. The prince moved away abruptly, and Hannah was finally able to draw a breath and rise to her feet.

"I'll be right back," she said, and retreated as quickly as her still-quivering legs would allow.

Michael sank back into his chair, then turned to face his daughter. He wasn't sure if he was angry or frustrated or grateful, and decided his feelings were probably a mixture of all those emotions—and several others he wasn't ready to acknowledge.

"Well, you've certainly made an impression today," he told Riley.

"I'm thirsty," she said again.

"Hannah gave you milk," he told her, trying to be patient. "And you spilled it all over the table and all over Hannah."

"I don't want milk, I want juice."

"You always have milk with dinner."

"I want juice," she insisted.

Though he had misgivings, he got up to get her drink. As he poured the juice into another cup, Hannah's words echoed in the back of his mind. *If you give in on all of the little things, she'll expect you to give in on the not-so-little things and then, suddenly, you have no authority anymore.*

He knew that she was right, and it irritated him that after less than a week with his daughter, Hannah had a better understanding of the child's needs than he did after almost four years. But the truth was, as much as he wanted to be a good father, he'd felt awkward and uncomfortable in the role from the very beginning. He'd constantly second-guessed everything he said and did around Riley, and whether it was a result of his ineptitude or not he knew Hannah was right: his daughter was turning into a pint-size dictator.

It was as if he was missing some kind of parenting gene—or maybe he'd deliberately suppressed it. When he and Sam got married, he knew that any pregnancy would be high-risk because of her diabetes and accepted that they might never have children. When she got pregnant, he'd been not only surprised but terrified. He knew what kind of risks she was facing, and he'd been so focused on her that he hadn't let himself think about the baby she carried.

Now that baby was almost four years old, the only caregivers she'd ever known were gone, and he'd hired a high school teacher to play nanny while he buried himself in his work, unwilling to even play at being a father. Was it any surprise that his daughter was acting out?

"Where's my juice?" she asked again when he returned to the table empty-handed.

"You can have juice with breakfast," he told her, trying to maintain a patient and reasonable tone.

"Now." She kicked her feet against the table.

"If you don't stop this right now, you'll have to go to bed without anything to eat or drink," Michael warned.

"You can't do that," Riley said, though there was a note of uncertainty in her voice now.

"I can and I will," he assured her.

His heart nearly broke when she started to cry again.

"It's Hannah's fault," she wailed. "She's making you be mean to me."

"Maybe, instead of always looking to blame someone else when you don't get your own way, you should start taking some responsibility for your own actions," he suggested.

She stared at him, completely baffled. He knew it wasn't because she didn't understand what he was saying but because the concept was completely foreign to her—because he had never before let there be consequences for her misbehavior. Instead, he'd made excuses—so many excuses, because she was a little girl without a mother.

While Riley considered what he'd said, Michael tried to tidy up the mess his daughter had made. He used another napkin to mop most of the spilled wine off of Hannah's plate, which made him recall the tantalizing image of the merlot spreading across her shirt, and the round fullness of the spectacular breasts beneath that shirt, and the blood in his head began to flow south.

He scowled as he righted her overturned goblet and refilled it. It had been a long time since he'd become aroused by nothing more than a mental image, and a lot longer since he'd been affected by a mental image of anyone other than Sam. He felt betrayed by his body's instinctive response to this woman, guilty that he could want a woman who wasn't his wife.

He knew that having sex with someone else wouldn't mean he was unfaithful. Sam was gone—he was no longer her husband but a widower. But he'd loved her for so long that even the thought of being with someone else felt like a betrayal of everything they'd shared and all the years they'd been together.

By the time Hannah returned to the table, the steaks and potatoes were cold. He offered to throw her plate in the microwave, but she insisted that it was fine. He didn't bother to heat his own dinner, either. He was too preoccupied wondering about the flavor of her lips to taste any of the food that he put in his mouth.

He'd been so tempted to kiss her. When he'd been crouched down beside her chair, his mouth only inches from hers, he'd very nearly leaned forward to breach the meager distance between them.

He didn't think she would have objected. It might have been a lot of years since he'd sent or received any kind of signals, but he was fairly certain that the attraction he felt wasn't one-sided. He was also fairly certain that he'd never experienced an attraction as sharp or intense as what he felt for Hannah Castillo.

He and Sam had been friends for a long time before they'd become lovers; their relationship had blossomed slowly and rooted deep. What he felt for Hannah was simple lust, basic yet undeniable.

It seemed disloyal to make any kind of comparison between the two women. Sam had been his partner in so many ways and the woman he loved with his whole heart; Hannah was a stranger on the periphery of his life, his daughter's temporary nanny—and the woman with whom he was going to be living in close quarters for the next two months. And he was definitely tempted to take advantage of that proximity.

"Are you hungry now?"

Though she wasn't speaking to him, Hannah's question interrupted his musings. Forcing his attention back to the table, he noticed that Riley was eyeing the plate Hannah had prepared for her, this time with more interest than irritation.

"If you dump it again, you won't have any dinner left," Hannah warned before she set the meal in front of the child.

His daughter immediately picked up a piece of potato and put it in her mouth.

"Use your fork, Riley," Michael said.

She didn't look at him, but she did pick up the fork and

speared a wedge of tomato. It was obvious that she was still angry with him, but at least she was eating. Though he'd tried to sound firm when he'd threatened to send her to bed without any dinner, he wasn't entirely sure he would have been able to follow through on his threat.

When the meal was finally over, Riley had eaten most of her potato and picked at the salad, but she'd adamantly refused to touch the steak.

"Dinner was excellent," Hannah said, pushing her chair away from the table. "Thank you."

"You're welcome," he replied, just as formally.

"I'll clean up the kitchen after I get Riley ready for bed," she told him. "And then, if you've got some time, I'd like to talk to you about a few things."

Michael nodded, though he wasn't certain he wanted to hear what Hannah was going to say. He was even less certain that he should be alone with the nanny without the buffer of his daughter between them.

Chapter Six

Riley had made it clear to her new nanny that she was neither needed nor wanted, and as Hannah finished tidying up the kitchen after the princess was tucked in bed, she began to question her true purpose for being at Cielo del Norte. Maybe she was being paranoid, but when she finally cornered the prince in his office, the first question that sprang to her mind was "Did my uncle ask you to fabricate a job for me so that I wouldn't go to China?"

The prince steepled his fingers over the papers on his desk. "I didn't know anything about your plans to go to China," he assured her. "And this job is most definitely not a fabrication."

She had no reason to distrust his response, but she still felt as if he could have hired a local high school student to do what she was doing—and for a lot less money. "But Riley's instructors spend more time with her than I do," she pointed out to him, "which makes me wonder why I'm even here."

"You're here to ensure that the status quo is maintained."

"Your daughter needs more than a supervisor, Your Highness. And if you can't see that, then I'm wasting my time."

He leaned back in his chair, his brows lifted in silent challenge. "After less than a week, you think you're an expert on what my daughter needs?"

"I don't need to be an expert to know that a child needs love more than she needs lessons," she assured him.

"Riley isn't a typical four-year-old," the prince pointed out.

"Maybe she's not typical, but she is only four."

"She is also both gifted and royal, and she has a lot to learn in order to fulfill the duties and responsibilities that will be required of her in the future."

"In the future," she acknowledged. "But right now, knowing how to make friends is more important than speaking French."

"I disagree."

"I'm not surprised," she said, and couldn't resist adding, "but then, you probably speak impeccable French."

His gaze narrowed. "Is there a point to this conversation, Miss Castillo?"

His tone—undeniably royal-to-servant—gave her pause. She hadn't been sure how far she intended to push, but in light of his apparent refusal to give any consideration to her opinions, she felt that she had no choice but to make him face some hard truths. Even if those truths cost her this job.

"I took Riley into town yesterday afternoon," she said, then hastened to reassure him—though with an undisguised note of sarcasm in her tone—"Don't worry. We weren't gone any longer than the allotted two hours of free time."

"Did Rafe go with you?" he demanded.

She nodded, confirming the presence of the security guard whose job it was to protect the princess whenever she went out in public. Although Riley was young enough to be of little interest to the paparazzi, there was always the possibility of encountering overzealous royal watchers or, worse, a kidnapper.

"Where did you go?"

"To the bookstore."

The furrow between his brows eased. "Riley enjoys visiting the bookstore."

"Right inside the door was a display case for a new book she wanted, but the case was empty. Then Riley spotted another child at the cash register with a copy in her hands. When I told Riley it was probably the last one, she tried to snatch it out of the other girl's hands."

"She is used to getting what she wants when she wants it," he admitted a little sheepishly.

"Because you give her what she wants when she wants it," she pointed out. "And it's turning her into a spoiled brat."

"Miss Castillo!"

She ignored the reprimand, because as angry as he was with her, she was still angrier about Riley's behavior the previous afternoon.

"And when the child counted out her money and realized she was two dollars short, Riley actually smirked at her—until I gave the extra two dollars to the clerk so the other girl could take it home, and then the princess threw a tantrum like I've never seen before."

Michael scrubbed his hands over his face as he considered his response. "Riley's status as a royal combined with her exceptional talents make it difficult for her to relate to children her own age," he finally said.

"Her behavior has nothing to do with her blue blood or superior IQ and everything to do with her sense of entitlement."

"If this arrangement isn't working out for you, maybe we should consider terminating our agreement," he suggested in an icy tone.

She shook her head. "I'm not quitting, and I don't think you really want to fire me."

"I wouldn't bet on that," he warned.

"If you were sincere about wanting someone to help with Riley, then you need me," she told him. "You might not want to admit it, but you do."

His brows rose imperiously. "Do you really think so?"

"I doubt you'd have much difficulty replacing me," she acknowledged. "I'm sure you could find someone who is willing to step in and manage Riley's schedule and defer to her every command, and at the end of the summer, you and your daughter would be exactly where you are now."

"I'm not seeing the downside."

Hannah had never doubted that the princess came by her attitude honestly enough. She forced herself to draw in a deep breath, then let it out slowly. She was a commoner and he was a royal and her bluntness bordered on rudeness, but someone needed to shake up his comfortable little world to make him see the bigger picture—for his sake, and certainly his daughter's.

"The downside is that, if you let this continue, the princess's behavior will be that much more difficult to correct later on," she told him.

"Don't you think you're overreacting to one little incident?"

"If it was only one little incident, I might agree, Your Highness. But you saw how she was at dinner. And I suspect that her behavior has been escalating for a long time."

"Do you really think she knocked your wineglass over on purpose?" His tone was filled with skepticism.

"I believe that she was acting out of frustration, because she's so accustomed to getting her own way that she doesn't know how to cope when she doesn't."

He was silent for a moment, as if he was actually considering her words. And when he spoke, his question gave her hope that he had finally heard what she was saying. "So what am I supposed to do?"

"You need to make some changes." She spoke gently but firmly.

"What kind of changes?" he asked warily.

Before Hannah could respond, his BlackBerry buzzed.

"That's the first one," she said, as he automatically unclipped the device from his belt to check the display.

"It's my secretary. I have to—"

"You have to stop putting your business before your daughter."

"That statement is neither fair nor accurate," he told her, as the phone buzzed again. "There is nothing more important to me than my daughter."

"And yet, when I'm trying to talk to you about her, it's killing you not to take that call, isn't it?"

Even as he shook his head in denial, his gaze dropped to the instrument again.

"Answer the phone, Your Highness." She turned toward the door. "I'll set up an appointment to continue this discussion when it's more convenient for you."

Hannah's words were still echoing in the back of his mind while Michael gathered the files and documents that he needed for his meetings in Port Augustine. He didn't expect her to understand how important his business was, why he felt the need to keep such a close eye on all of the details.

He did it for himself—the business was a way to be self-supporting rather than living off of his title and inheritance, and it was something to keep him busy while his daughter was occupied with her numerous lessons and activities. He also did it for Sam—to ensure that the business they'd built together continued not just to survive but to thrive. And while it did, his sense of satisfaction was bittersweet because his wife wasn't around to celebrate with him.

Ironically, the company's success was one of the reasons that Sam had been anxious to start a family. The business didn't need her anymore, she'd claimed, but a baby would. Michael had assured her that he still needed her, and she'd smiled and promised to always be there for him. But she'd lied. She'd given birth to their daughter, and then she'd abandoned both of them.

He knew that she would never have chosen to leave them, that she would never have wanted Riley to grow up without a mother. But that knowledge had done little to ease his grief, and so he'd buried himself in his work, as if keeping his mind and his hands occupied could make his heart ache for her less.

Except that he rarely did any hands-on work himself anymore, aside from occasional projects for a few of the firm's original clients, his pro bono work for the National Diabetes Association and a few other charitable causes. For the most part, he supervised his employees and worked his connections to bring in new clients. And although he'd claimed that he was too busy to take a two-month vacation, the truth was, he could easily do so and know that his business was in good hands. The knowledge should have filled him with pride and satisfaction, but he only felt…empty.

Truthfully, his greatest pride was his daughter. She was also his biggest concern. After almost four years, he felt as if he was still trying to find his way with her. Their relationship would be different, he was certain, if Sam had been around. Everything would be different if Sam was still around.

Your daughter needs more than a nanny—she needs a mother.

He knew it was probably true. But he had no intention

of marrying again just to give Riley a mother. He had no intention of marrying again, period.

You are still young—you have many years to live, much love to give.

While he appreciated Caridad's faith in him, he wasn't sure that was true. He'd given his whole heart to Sam—and when he'd lost her, he'd been certain that there wasn't anything left to share with anyone else.

Of course, Riley had changed that. He'd never understood the all-encompassing love of a parent for a child until he'd held his baby girl in his arms. And as Riley had grown, so had the depth and breadth of his feelings for her. But knowing what to do with a baby didn't come as instinctively as the loving, and for the first year of her life, he'd relied on Marissa and Brigitte to tend to most of Riley's needs.

And then, just when he'd thought he was getting the hang of fatherhood, he'd realized that Riley needed so much more than he could give her. So he made sure that there were people around to meet her needs—tutors and caregivers—and he turned his focus back to his business.

When he told Hannah about his intended trip back to Port Augustine after lunch on Sunday, she just nodded, as if she wasn't at all surprised that he was leaving. Of course, she probably wasn't. She'd made it more than clear the previous night that she thought he valued RAM above all else. While that wasn't anywhere close to being the truth, he wasn't prepared to walk away from the company, either.

"I'm the president and CEO," the prince reminded her. "Fulfilling those positions requires a lot of work and extended hours at the office."

"I didn't ask, Your Highness," she said evenly.

"No, you'd rather disapprove than understand."

"Maybe because I can't understand why you don't want to spend any time with your daughter," she admitted.

"It's not a question of want."

"Isn't it?" she challenged.

He frowned. "Of course not."

"Because it seems to me that a man who is the president and CEO of his own company—not to mention a member of the royal family—would be able to delegate some of his responsibilities."

"I do delegate," he insisted. "But ultimately, I'm the one who's responsible."

"But it's your wife's name on the door, isn't it?"

"What does that have to do with anything?"

She shrugged. "Maybe nothing. Maybe everything."

"Could you be a little more indecisive?" he asked dryly.

"I just can't help wondering if your obsession with the business isn't really about holding on to the last part of the woman you loved."

"That's ridiculous," he said, startled as much by the bluntness of the statement as the accusation.

"I agree," she said evenly. "Because the business isn't the only part you have left of your wife. It's not even the best part—your daughter is."

"And my daughter is the reason you're here," he reminded her. "So you should focus on taking care of her and not lecturing me."

She snapped her mouth shut. "You're right."

"Especially when you couldn't be more off base."

"I apologized for speaking candidly, but I was only speaking the truth as I see it, Your Highness."

"Then your vision is skewed," he insisted.

"Maybe it is," she allowed.

"The potential client is only going to be in town a few days," he said, wanting to make her understand. "If the meeting goes well, it could turn into a big contract for RAM."

"What would happen if you skipped the meeting?" she challenged. "Or let one of your associates handle it instead?"

"The client specifically asked to deal with me."

"And if you said you were unavailable?"

"We would lose the account," he told her.

"And then what?" she pressed.

He frowned. "What do you mean?"

"Would you miss a mortgage payment? Would the bank foreclose on your home?"

"Of course not, but—"

"But somehow this meeting is more important than the vacation you're supposed to be sharing with your daughter?"

She was wrong, of course. But he could see how it appeared that way, from her perspective.

"The timing of the meeting is unfortunate and unchangeable," he told her, "which is why you're here to take care of Riley in my absence."

"Don't you think it would be better if Riley had more than a week to get to know me before you left?"

"I agree the circumstances aren't ideal," he acknowledged. "But I trust that you can manage for a few days."

That was apparently her job—to manage. While her lack of experience had given her some concern about taking a job as a nanny, Hannah had sincerely looked forward to spending time with the young princess. But the truth was, she spent less time with Riley than did any of the little girl's instructors.

And while she rarely saw the prince outside of mealtimes, their weekend beach outing aside, just knowing he had gone back to Port Augustine somehow made the house seem emptier, lonelier. Or maybe it was the weather that was responsible for her melancholy mood. The day was gray and rainy, Riley was busy with one of her countless lessons, leaving Hannah on her own.

After wandering the halls for a while—she'd spent hours just exploring and admiring the numerous rooms of Cielo del Norte—she decided to spend some time with Caridad.

Although she'd only been at the house for a week, she'd gotten to know the housekeeper quite well and enjoyed talking with her. But Caridad was up to her elbows in dough with flour all over the counters, so she shooed Hannah out of her way.

Hannah felt as if she should be doing something, but when she finally accepted that there was nothing she *had* to do and considered what she *wanted* to do instead, she headed for the library.

It was, admittedly, her absolute favorite space in the whole house. She had always been a voracious reader, and on her first visit to the room she'd been thrilled to find that the floor-to-ceiling bookcases were stocked with an eclectic assortment of materials. There were essays and biographies; textbooks and travel guides; volumes of short stories, poetry and plays; there were leather-bound classics, hardback copies of current bestsellers and dog-eared paperbacks. She spent several minutes just perusing the offerings, until a recent title by one of her favorite thriller writers caught her eye.

She settled into the antique camelback sofa with her feet tucked up under her and cracked open the cover. As always, the author's storytelling technique drew her right in, and her heart was already pounding in anticipation as the killer approached his next victim when a knock sounded on the door.

The knock was immediately followed by the entrance of a visitor and, with a startled gasp, Hannah jumped to her feet and dropped a quick—and probably awkward—curtsy.

"I beg your pardon, Your Highness, you caught me—"

"In the middle of a good book," the princess finished with a smile, as she offered her hand. "I'm Marissa Leandres, Michael's sister."

Of course, Hannah had recognized her immediately. Although the princess kept a rather low profile and wasn't a usual target of the paparazzi, she made frequent public appearances for her favorite charities and causes.

"I recently read that one myself and couldn't put it down," Marissa admitted. "So if I'm interrupting a good part, please tell me so, and I'll take my tea in the kitchen with Caridad."

"Of course not," Hannah lied, because after being banished by the housekeeper, the prospect of actual human company was even more enticing than the book still in her hand.

"Good," the princess said, settling into a balloon-back chair near the sofa. "Because I would love for you to join me, if you have a few minutes to spare."

"I have a lot more minutes to spare than I would have anticipated when I took this job," Hannah admitted.

The other woman's smile was wry. "I guess that means that my brother, once again, chose to ignore my advice."

"What was your advice?"

"To give Riley a break from her lessons, at least for the summer."

"So I'm not the only one who thinks that her schedule is a little over the top for a not-quite-four-year-old?" Even as the words spilled out of her mouth, Hannah winced, recognizing the inappropriateness of criticizing a member of the royal family—and to his sister, no less.

"Please don't censor your thoughts on my account," Marissa said. "And I absolutely agree with you about Riley's schedule. Although, in his defence, Michael believes he is doing what's best for Riley."

"I'm sure he does," she agreed, even if she still disagreed with his decision to leave Cielo del Norte—and his daughter. Thinking of that now, she apologized to the princess. "And I'm sure the prince must not have known of your plans to visit today because he went back to Port Augustine this morning."

Marissa waved a hand. "I didn't come to see him, anyway. I came to meet you. And I would have come sooner, but I've been tied up in meetings at the hospital, trying to get final approval for the expansion of the neonatal department at PACH."

"The Juno Project."

Marissa smiled. "Of course you would know about it—your uncle has been one of my staunchest allies on the board."

"He believes very strongly in what you're doing."

"Don't encourage me," the princess warned. "Because if I start talking about what we want to do, I won't be able to stop, and that really isn't why I'm here."

Another knock on the door preceded Caridad's entrance. She pushed a fancy cart set with a silver tea service, elegant gold-rimmed cups and saucers, and a plate of freshly baked scones with little pots of jam and clotted cream.

"Thank you," Marissa said to the housekeeper. "Those scones look marvelous."

Though she didn't actually smile, Caridad looked pleased by the compliment. "Would you like me to serve, Your Highness?"

"No, I think we can handle it."

"Very well then." She bobbed a curtsy and exited the room, closing the door again behind her.

"She makes that curtsying thing look so easy," Hannah mused. "I always feel like I'm going to tip over."

Marissa smiled as she poured the tea.

"It does take some practice," she agreed. "But I wouldn't worry about it. We don't stand on ceremony too much in my family—well, none of us but my mother. And it's not likely you'll have occasion to cross paths with her while you're here."

The statement piqued Hannah's curiosity, but she didn't feel it was her place to ask and, thankfully, the princess didn't seem to expect a response.

"So how are you getting along with my brother?" Marissa asked, passing a cup of tea to her.

"I don't really see a lot of the prince," Hannah admitted.

"Is he hiding out in his office all the time?"

"He's working in his office all of the time," she clarified.

"He does have the National Diabetes Awareness Campaign coming up in the fall," the princess acknowledged. "He always gives that a lot of time and attention—and pro bono, too."

Her surprise must have shown on her face, because Marissa said, "I know Michael sometimes acts like it's all about making money, but he does a lot of work for charities—Literacy, Alzheimer's, the Cancer Society—and never bills for it."

Hannah knew that his wife had been diabetic, so she should have expected that awareness of the disease was a cause close to his heart, but she hadn't expected to learn that he had such a kind and generous heart.

"I didn't know he did any of that," she admitted.

"Michael doesn't think it's a big deal," the princess confided. "But giving back is important to him. After Sam died...I don't know how much you know about his history, but he went through a really tough time then."

"I can't even begin to imagine," Hannah murmured.

"Neither can I," Marissa confided, "and I was there. I saw how losing her completely tore him apart—nearly decimated him. I tried to be understanding, but I don't think anyone really can understand the magnitude of that kind of grief without having experienced the kind of love that he and Sam shared.

"It took him a long time to see through the fog of that grief—to see Riley. But when he finally did, he put all of his efforts into being a good father to his little girl. He prepared her bottles, he changed her diapers, he played peekaboo."

As hard as Hannah tried, she couldn't imagine the prince

she'd only started to get to know over the past week doing any of those things. While it was obvious that he loved his daughter, it seemed just as obvious to Hannah that he was more comfortable with her at a distance.

"He made mistakes, as all new parents do, but he figured things out as he went along. Then he found out that Riley was gifted, and everything changed."

"Why?"

"Because Michael was just starting to find his way as a father when one of the specialists suggested that Riley would benefit from more structured activities, as if what he was doing wasn't enough. So he asked Brigitte to set up some interviews with music teachers and language instructors and academic tutors, and suddenly Riley's day became one lesson after another. Honestly, her schedule for the past six months has been more intense than mine."

While Hannah doubted that was true, she did think the princess's insight might explain Riley's bed-wetting episode. It wasn't that the little girl was regressing to her toddler habits, just that the signal of her body's need hadn't been able to overcome the absolute exhaustion of her mind.

"I think that's when he started spending longer hours at the office, because he felt like Riley didn't need him."

"I've tried to talk to the prince about his daughter's schedule," Hannah admitted now. "But he seems...resistant."

The princess's brows lifted. "Are you always so diplomatic?"

She flushed, recalling too many times when she'd freely spoken her mind, as if forgetting not just that he was a prince but also her boss. "I'm sure His Highness would say not."

Marissa laughed. "Then I will say that I'm very glad you're here. My brother needs someone in his life who isn't afraid to speak her mind."

"I'm only here for the summer," Hannah reminded her.

"That just might be long enough," Marissa said with a secretive smile.

Hannah didn't dare speculate about what the princess's cryptic comment could mean.

Chapter Seven

It was ten o'clock by the time Michael left the restaurant Tuesday night, but he did so with the knowledge that the prospective clients were going to sign a contract at nine o'clock the following morning. He didn't need to be there for that part of things—he'd done his job, gotten the client's verbal commitment; the rest was just paperwork. The documents had already been prepared by his secretary and the signing would be witnessed by the company vice president, so there was no reason that Michael couldn't head back to Cielo del Norte right now. True, it would be after midnight before he arrived, but he wasn't tired. In fact, the drive would give him a chance to let him unwind.

But for some reason, he found himself following the familiar route toward his home in Verde Colinas.

He unlocked the door but didn't bother turning on any lights as he walked through the quiet of the now-empty house toward his bedroom. It was the bedroom he'd shared with his wife during their twelve-year marriage. Even the bed was the same, and there were still nights that he'd roll over and reach for her—and wake with an ache in the heart that was as empty as his arms.

For months after she'd gone, he could still smell her perfume every time he walked into their bedroom. It was as if her very essence had permeated every item in the room. Each time, the scent had been like a kick to the gut—a constant reminder that while her fragrance might linger, his wife was gone.

He wasn't sure when that sense of her had finally faded, but now he was desperate for it, for some tangible reminder of the woman he'd loved. He drew in a deep breath, but all he could smell was fresh linen and lemon polish.

He stripped away his clothes and draped them over the chair beside the bed, then pulled back the covers and crawled between the cool sheets.

He deliberately shifted closer to Sam's side of the bed, and he was thinking of her as he drifted to sleep.

But he dreamed of Hannah.

The prince had told Hannah that he would probably be away overnight, but he was gone for three days.

At first, despite the nightly phone calls to his daughter, it didn't seem as if Riley was even aware of her father's absence. But then Hannah noticed the subtle changes in the little girl's behavior. She went about her daily routines, but she was unusually quiet and compliant at mealtimes, and she wet her bed both nights. The first morning that Hannah saw the damp sheets in a heap on the floor, she waited for Riley's tirade. But the little girl only asked if she had time to take a bath before breakfast.

By Wednesday, Hannah was desperate for something—anything—to cheer up the little girl. It was the only day of the week that Riley's lessons were finished by lunchtime, so in the morning, she dialed the familiar number of her best friend.

"I'm calling at a bad time," she guessed, when she registered the sound of crying in the background.

"Gabriel's teething," Karen replied wearily. "It's always a bad time."

"Maybe I can help," Hannah suggested.

"Unless you want to take the kid off of my hands for a few hours so I can catch up on my sleep, I doubt it."

"I was actually hoping to take Grace off of your hands for a few hours, but I might be able to handle the baby, too."

She must have sounded as uncertain as she felt, because Karen managed a laugh. "The new nanny gig must be a piece of cake if you want to add more kids to the mix."

"I wouldn't say it's been a piece of cake," Hannah confided. "But I really would appreciate it if Grace could come over and hang out with Riley for a while."

The only response was, aside from the background crying, complete and utter silence.

"Karen?" she prompted.

"I'm sorry. I'm just a little—a lot—surprised. I mean, Grace is a great kid, but she goes to public school."

Hannah laughed. "She is a great kid, and I think it would be great for Riley to play with someone closer to her own age." Although her friend's daughter had just turned six and the princess wasn't quite four, Hannah didn't have any concerns about Riley being able to keep up with Grace. "So—will you come?"

"I'm packing Gabe's diaper bag as we speak," Karen assured her.

"Could you bring some of Grace's toys and games, too?"

"Sure. What does the princess like to play with?"

"That's what I'm trying to figure out," Hannah admitted.

For the first time since Hannah arrived at Cielo del Norte, she felt as if she and Riley had a really good day. Of course, it was really Grace's visit that made the difference for the princess. After Riley got past her initial hesitation about meeting someone new, the two girls had a wonderful time together. They played some board games, made sculptures with modeling clay, built towers of blocks—which Gabe happily knocked down for them—and sang and danced in the music room. The adults observed without interference until Grace suggested playing hide-and-seek, then Karen insisted on limiting their game to only four rooms, to ensure that her daughter didn't wander off too far and get lost.

Hannah was amazed by the transformation of the princess into a normal little girl. And while Karen still looked like she would benefit from a good night of uninterrupted sleep, she thanked Hannah for the invite, insisting that the change of venue and adult conversation were just what she needed to feel human again. For her part, Hannah was happy to have the time with her friend—and thrilled to cuddle with ten-month-old Gabe.

"Did you have fun playing with Grace today?" Hannah asked when she tucked Riley into bed later that night.

The princess nodded. "Her mommy is very pretty."

The wistful tone in her voice made Hannah's heart ache for the little girl who didn't have any memories of her own mother. "Yes, she is," she agreed. "Her mommy is also one of my best friends."

"I don't have a best friend," Riley admitted. "I don't have any friends at all."

"Only because you haven't had a chance to make friends. That will change when you go to school in September."

Riley looked away. "I don't want to go to school."

"Why not?"

The little girl shrugged. "Because I won't know anyone there."

"It can be scary," Hannah admitted. "Going new places,

meeting new people. But it's going to be new for all of the other kids, too."

"Really?"

"Really," Hannah assured her.

"When did you meet your best friend?" Riley wanted to know.

"The first year that I came to Tesoro del Mar to live with my uncle Phillip."

"He's my doctor," Riley said, then her little brow furrowed. "But why did you live with your uncle? Where was your daddy?"

Hannah thought it was telling—and more than a little sad—that Riley didn't ask about her mother. Because, in her experience, it was more usual for little girls to live with their daddies than with both of their parents.

"My daddy lived far away."

"Why didn't you live with him there?"

"I used to," Hannah told her. "Before my mother died."

The princess's eyes went wide. "Your mommy died, too?"

Hannah nodded. "When I was a few years older than you."

"Do you miss her?"

She nodded again. "Even though it was a very long time ago, I still miss her very much."

"I don't remember my mommy," Riley admitted, almost guiltily.

Hannah brushed a lock of hair off of the little girl's forehead. "You couldn't," she said gently, hoping to reassure her. "You were only a baby when she died."

"But I have a present from her."

"What's that?"

The princess pointed to the beautifully dressed silken-haired doll on the top of her tallest dresser. Hannah had noticed it the first time she'd ever ventured into the room, partly because it was so exquisite and partly because it was the only doll the little girl seemed to own.

"I call her Sara."

After the little princess in the story by Frances Hodgson Burnett, Hannah guessed, having seen a copy of the book on Riley's shelf of favorites.

"That's a very pretty name," she said. "For a very pretty doll."

The child smiled shyly. "Daddy said she looks just like my mommy, when she was a little girl. And he put her up there so that she could always watch over me." Then she sighed.

"Why does that make you sad?" Hannah asked her.

"I just think that she must be lonely, because she has no one to play with."

"Are you lonely?"

Riley shook her head, though the denial seemed more automatic than sincere, and her gaze shifted toward the doll again. "There's always a teacher or someone with me."

"You are very busy with your lessons." Hannah took Sara off of the dresser, smoothed a hand over her springy blond curls. The princess watched her every move, seemingly torn between shock and pleasure that her beloved Sara had been moved from her very special place. Hannah straightened the velvet skirt, then adjusted the bow on one of her black boots, and finally offered the doll to Riley.

The child's eyes went wide, and for a moment Hannah thought she might shake her head, refusing the offer. But then her hand reached out and she tentatively touched a finger to the lace that peeked out from beneath the doll's full skirt.

"But maybe you could spend some time with Sara when you're not too busy?"

She nodded, not just an affirmation but a promise, and hugged the doll against her chest.

"And maybe Grace could come back to play another time," Hannah continued.

The last of the shadows lifted from the little girl's eyes. "Do you think she would?"

"I think she'd be happy to." She pulled the covers up to Riley's chin. "Good night."

"'Night," Riley echoed, her eyes already drifting shut.

Hannah switched off the lamp on the bedside table and started to tiptoe out of the room.

"Hannah?"

She paused at the door. "Did you need something?"

There was a slight hesitation, and then Riley finally said, "Daddy sometimes sits with me until I fall asleep."

And as Michael hadn't been home for the past two nights, his daughter was obviously missing him. "I'm not sure when your daddy's going to be home," she admitted, because he never spoke to her when he called except to ask for his daughter and she hadn't felt entitled to inquire about his agenda.

"Could you stay for a while?" Riley asked. "Please?"

"I would be happy to stay," Hannah told her.

The princess's lips curved, just a little. "You don't have to stay long. I'm very tired."

"I'll stay as long as you want," she promised.

Hannah wasn't very tired herself, but the night was so dark and quiet that she found her eyes beginning to drift shut. She thought about going across the hall to her own bed, but she didn't want to tiptoe away until she was certain that Riley wouldn't awaken. So she listened to the soft, even sounds of the little girl's breathing...

Michael had stayed away longer than he'd intended, and he was feeling more than a little guilty about his extended absence. And angry at himself when he finally recognized the real reason behind his absence—he'd been hiding.

His sister would probably say that he'd been hiding from life the past four years, and maybe that was true to a certain extent. But for the past three days, he'd been hiding from something else—or rather some*one* else: Hannah Castillo.

Since she'd moved into Cielo del Norte, she'd turned his entire life upside down. She made him question so many things he'd been certain of, and she made him feel too many things he didn't want to feel.

After two long, sleepless nights alone in his bed in Verde Colinas, he'd accepted that he couldn't keep hiding forever.

Besides, he missed his daughter, and hearing her voice on the phone couldn't compare to feeling the warmth of her arms around his neck.

Whether Hannah believed it or not, Riley was the center of his world. Maybe he spent more hours in his office than he did with his child, but it was the time he spent with her that made every day worthwhile. It was her smile that filled the dark places in his heart with light, and her laughter that lifted his spirits when nothing else could.

Even now, as he tiptoed toward her room, his step was lighter because he was finally home with her.

Of course, being home also meant being in close proximity to Hannah again, but he was confident that he would figure out a way to deal with the unwelcome feelings she stirred inside of him. And anyway, that wasn't something he was going to worry about before morning.

Or so he thought until he stepped into Riley's room and saw her in the chair beside his daughter's bed.

He stopped abruptly, and her eyelids flickered, then slowly lifted.

"What are you doing here?" Though he'd spoken in a whisper, the words came out more harshly than he'd intended.

Hannah blinked, obviously startled by the sharp demand. "Riley asked me to sit with her until she fell asleep."

"I would hope she's been asleep for a while," he told her. "It's after midnight."

"I guess I fell asleep, too."

"You should be in your own bed," he told her.

She nodded and eased out of the chair.

He moved closer, to adjust Riley's covers. As he pulled up the duvet, he noticed that there was something tucked beneath her arm. He felt a funny tug in his belly as he recognized the doll that Sam had bought when she learned that she was having a baby girl.

It was the only thing Riley had that was chosen specifically for her by her mother. Now its dress was rumpled and its hair was in disarray and one of its boots was falling off. He tried to ease the doll from Riley's grasp, but as soon as he tried to wriggle it free, her arm tightened around it. With a sigh of both regret and resignation, he left the doll with his daughter and caught up with Hannah outside of the room.

He grabbed her arm to turn her around to face him. "What were you thinking?" he demanded, the words ground out between clenched teeth.

The nanny blinked, startled by his evident fury, and yanked her arm away from him. "I don't know what you're talking about, Your Highness, but if you're going to yell at me, you might not want to do so right outside of your daughter's bedroom."

He acknowledged her suggestion with a curt nod. "Downstairs."

Her eyes narrowed, and for just a second he thought she would balk at the command. Maybe he wanted her to balk. Her defiance would give him a reason to hold on to his fury, because touching Hannah—even just his hand on her arm— had turned his thoughts in a whole other direction. But then she moved past him and started down the stairs.

She paused at the bottom, as if uncertain of where to go from there.

"My office," he told her.

She went through the door, then turned to face him, her arms folded over her chest. "Now could you please explain what's got you all twisted up in knots?"

"The doll in Riley's bed."

He saw the change in her eyes, the shift from confusion to understanding. Then her chin lifted. "What about it?"

"It's not a toy."

"Dolls are meant to be played with," she told him firmly.

"Not that one."

She shook her head. "You don't even realize what you're doing, do you?"

"What *I'm* doing?" he demanded incredulously, wondering how she could possibly turn this around so that it was his fault.

"Yes, what *you're* doing. You told Riley this wonderful story about how her mother picked out the doll just for her, then you put it on a shelf where she couldn't reach it, so that the only tangible symbol she has of her mother stayed beautiful but untouchable."

He scowled at her. "That's not what I did at all."

"Maybe it's not what you intended, Your Highness," she said in a more gentle tone, "but it's what happened."

He'd only wanted to preserve the gift for Riley so that she would have it forever. But he realized now that Hannah was right, that in doing so he'd ensured that she didn't really have it at all.

He shook his head, the last of his anger draining away, leaving only weariness and frustration. "Am I ever going to get anything right?"

He felt her touch on his arm. "You're doing a lot of things right."

He looked down at her hand, at the long, slender fingers that were so pale against his darker skin, and marveled that she would try to comfort him after the way he'd attacked her. She truly was a remarkable woman. Strong enough to stand up to him, yet soft enough to offer comfort.

"That's not the tune you were singing the last time we discussed my daughter," he reminded her.

Her hand dropped away as one side of her mouth tipped up in a half smile. "I'm not saying that you're doing *everything* right," she teased. "But I do think you have a lot of potential."

"If I'm willing to make some changes," he said, remembering.

She nodded.

"Do you want to talk about those changes now or should we just go up to bed?"

He didn't realize how much the words sounded like an invitation until she stepped back. He didn't realize how tempted he was by the idea himself until he'd spoken the words aloud.

"I meant to say that if you're tired, you can go upstairs to your own bed," he clarified.

"Oh. Of course," she said, though he could tell by the color in her cheeks that she had been thinking of something else entirely. Unfortunately, he couldn't tell if she was intrigued or troubled by the something else.

"I apologize for my poor word choice," he said. "I didn't mean to make you uncomfortable."

"You didn't."

He took a step closer to her, knowing that he was close to stepping over a line that he shouldn't but too tempted by this woman to care. "You didn't think I was propositioning you?"

"Of course not," she denied, though her blush suggested otherwise.

"Why 'of course not'?" he asked curiously.

She dropped her gaze. "Because a man like you—a prince—would never be interested in someone like me."

There was a time when he'd thought he would never be interested in anyone who wasn't Sam, but the past ten days had proven otherwise. Even when he wasn't near Hannah, he was thinking about her, wanting her. He knew that he shouldn't, but that knowledge did nothing to diminish his desire.

"You're an attractive woman, Hannah. It would be a mistake to assume that any man would not be interested."

"You're confusing me," she admitted. "In one breath, you say that you're not propositioning me, and in the next, you say that you find me attractive."

"Actually, my comment was more objective than subjective," he told her. "But while I do think you're a very attractive woman, I didn't hire you in order to pursue a personal relationship with you."

"Okay," she said, still sounding wary.

Not that he could blame her. Because even as he was saying one thing, he was thinking something else entirely.

"In fact, I wouldn't have invited you to spend the summer here if I thought there was any danger of an attraction leading to anything else."

"Okay," she said again.

"I just want you to understand that I didn't intend for this to happen at all," he said, and slid his arms around her.

"What is happening?" she asked, a little breathlessly.

"This," he said.

And then he kissed her.

Chapter Eight

She hadn't anticipated the touch of his lips to hers.

Maybe it was because her head was already spinning, trying to follow the thread of their conversation. Or maybe it was because she would never, in a million years, have anticipated that Prince Michael might kiss her. But whatever the reason, Hannah was caught completely off guard when the prince's mouth pressed against hers.

Maybe she should have protested. Maybe she should have pushed him away. But the fact was, with the prince's deliciously firm and undeniably skillful lips moving over hers, she was incapable of coherent thought or rational response. And instead of protesting, she yielded; instead of pushing him away, she pressed closer.

It was instinct that caused her to lift her arms and link them behind his head, and desire—pure and simple—that had her lips parting beneath the coaxing pressure of his. Then his tongue brushed against hers, and everything inside of her quivered.

Had she ever been kissed like this? Wanted like this? She didn't know; she couldn't think. Nothing in her limited experience had prepared her for the masterful seduction of his lips. And when his hands skimmed over her, boldly sweeping down her back and over her buttocks, pulling her closer, she nearly melted into a puddle at his feet.

She couldn't have said how long the kiss lasted.

Minutes? Hours? Days?

It seemed like forever—and not nearly long enough.

When he finally eased his lips from hers, she nearly whimpered with regret.

Then she opened her eyes, and clearly saw the regret in his.

It was like a knife to the heart that only moments before had been bubbling over with joy. Being kissed by Prince Michael was, for Hannah, a dream come true. But for Prince Michael, kissing her had obviously been a mistake, a momentary error in judgment.

Her hand moved to her mouth, her fingertips trembling as they pressed against her still-tingling lips. Everything inside her was trembling, aching, yearning, even as he was visibly withdrawing.

"I'm sorry." He took another step back. "I shouldn't have done that."

He was right. Of course, he was right. What had happened—even if it was just a kiss—should never have happened. He was Riley's father and her employer. But, even more importantly, he was a prince and she was *not* a princess. She was nobody.

That was a lesson she should have learned years ago, when Harrison Parker had taken back his ring because she didn't have a pedigree deemed suitable by his family. But all it had taken was one touch from the prince, and she'd forgotten everything but how much she wanted him.

How had it happened? One minute they'd been arguing

and in the next he'd claimed that he was attracted to her. Then he'd kissed her as if he really wanted to. And when he'd held her close, his arms wrapped around her, his body pressed against hers, she'd had no doubt about his desire. But then he'd pulled away, making it clear that he didn't want to want her.

Proving, once again, that she simply wasn't good enough.

"Hannah?"

She had to blink away the tears that stung her eyes before she could look at him.

"Are you okay?"

The evident concern in his voice helped her to steel her spine. "I'm fine, Your Highness. It wasn't a big deal."

He frowned, and she wondered—for just a moment—if he might dispute her statement. If maybe he, too, felt that it *had* been a big deal.

But in the end, he only said, "I was way out of line. And I promise that you won't be subjected to any more unwanted advances."

"I'm not worried about that, Your Highness," she said confidently.

And she wasn't.

What worried her was that his kiss hadn't been unwanted at all.

He dreamed of her again.

Of course, this time the dream was much more vivid and real. And when Michael finally awakened in the morning with the sheets twisted around him, he knew that it was his own fault.

He never should have kissed her.

Not just because he'd stepped over the line, but because one simple kiss had left him wanting so much more.

It wasn't a big deal.

Maybe it wasn't to Hannah, but to Michael—who hadn't

kissed anyone but Sam since their first date so many years before—it was.

He didn't feel guilty, not really. His wife had been gone for almost four years, and he knew she would never have expected him to live the rest of his life as a monk. But he did feel awkward. If he was going to make a move on anyone, he should have chosen a woman he would not have to interact with on a daily basis from now until the end of the summer, and especially not an employee.

He winced as he imagined the headlines that a sexual harassment suit would generate, then realized he was probably being paranoid. After all, to Hannah the kiss "wasn't a big deal."

He would just have to make sure that he kept his promise, that absolutely nothing like that ever happened again. And count down the days until the end of the summer.

After Hannah ensured that Riley was wherever she needed to be for her first lesson of the day, she usually returned to the kitchen to enjoy another cup of Caridad's fabulous coffee and conversation with the longtime housekeeper of Cielo del Norte.

But when she approached the kitchen Thursday morning, she could hear that the other woman already had company—and from the tone of her voice, she wasn't too pleased with her visitor.

"This isn't open for discussion," Caridad said firmly.

"But it isn't fair—"

"Whoever said life was supposed to be fair?"

"You never made Jocelyn go to summer school," the male voice argued.

"Because Jocelyn didn't struggle with English Lit."

"She would have if she'd had Mr. Gaffe as her teacher."

"You complained about the teacher you had last year, now you complain about this teacher—maybe the problem isn't the teachers but the student. And maybe you should have paid a little more attention to the lessons and a little less to Serik Jouharian last term."

Based on the dialogue and the tones of their voices, Hannah guessed that Caridad was talking to her son. She knew that the housekeeper and her husband had five children—four girls and, finally, a boy. Kevin was the only one still living at home and, according to Caridad, he was responsible for every single one of her gray hairs.

"The only reason I even passed that course was because Serik was my study partner," the boy told her now.

"Then you'd better pick your study partner as carefully this time."

Hannah peeked around the corner in time to see Caridad kiss her son's cheek, then hand him his backpack. "Now go, so you're not late."

"Serik," Hannah said, as Kevin exited the room. "That's a beautiful name."

"Serik was a beautiful girl. An exchange student from Armenia, and I thanked God when school was done and she went back to her own country." Caridad sighed. "He was so smitten. And so heartbroken when she said goodbye."

"I guess he's at that age."

"The age when hormones lead to stupid?"

Hannah laughed. "He seems like a good kid."

"He is," Caridad admitted. "And smart. He's always got good marks in school, except for English. I thought if he took the next course at summer school, when he only has to focus on one subject, he might do better, but he's done nothing but complain since the course started."

"He's a teenager and it's the summer," Hannah said. "Of course he's going to complain about being stuck in school."

"He says he'd rather be working, and if I let him get a job, he could help pay for his education. But I worry that a job would take time away from his studies, jeopardizing his chances of getting a scholarship."

"I could tutor him," she offered.

"No offense, but I can't imagine that a nanny knows too much about senior English."

"You might have noticed that I don't know too much about being a nanny," she said. "That's because I'm a teacher in my real life."

"Your real life?"

"Well, nothing about this seems real to me." She looked around at the kitchen that was bigger than her whole apartment in the city. "It's as if I've fallen through the rabbit hole."

"Should we call you Alice?"

She smiled. "No. Riley's already confused enough without giving a new name to the new hire."

"So how did an English teacher end up taking a summer job as a royal nanny?"

"Desperation."

"Prince Michael's desperation or your own?"

"Both, I guess. He needed someone who could step in right away while he continues to look for a full-time caregiver, and I needed a job and a place to stay for the summer because I sublet my apartment with the intention of spending the break teaching in China." She shook her head in response to the lift of Caridad's brows. "Don't ask."

"We can't afford a tutor," Caridad admitted. "Prince Michael offered to hire one when he heard that Kevin was struggling, but I couldn't let him do that when he already does so much for us."

"I'm already getting a paycheck, and I really do love to teach."

"I wouldn't feel right—taking something for nothing."

"We could exchange services," Hannah suggested. "Maybe you could teach me to cook?"

"Not likely," the housekeeper said.

Hannah couldn't help but feel disappointed by her response. Cooking lessons would at least give her something to do while Riley was busy with her tutors, but unlike her, Caridad probably had more than enough to keep her busy.

"You don't think you'd have the time?" she guessed.

"I don't think you could learn," the older woman admitted bluntly. "You don't know the difference between browning and burning."

Hannah couldn't deny it was true—not when the housekeeper had asked her to keep an eye on the garlic bread while she put a load of laundry in the wash. All Hannah had to do was take the tray out of the oven when the cheese started to brown. But then Riley had come into the kitchen to get a drink and she'd spilled her juice, and while Hannah was busy mopping up the floor, the cheese was turning from brown to black.

"Don't you think that's a little unfair?" she asked, because she had explained the extenuating circumstances behind the mishap.

"Maybe," Caridad agreed. "But not untrue."

Hannah had to laugh. "No, not untrue," she admitted as she poured herself a fresh cup of coffee. "But is that any reason to let your son struggle?"

The housekeeper hesitated. "It's only the first week. I want to see him at least make an effort before you bail him out."

Hannah and Riley spent the following Saturday afternoon on the beach again, but the prince made no effort to join them. And although the three of them had dinner together, as usual, the prince immediately retreated to his office after the meal was done.

It was Monday before Hannah worked up the nerve to knock on his office door.

She could hear him talking, and she pictured him pacing

in front of his desk with his BlackBerry in hand. It seemed as if it was *always* in hand. His voice rose, as if to emphasize a point, and she took a step back. Maybe she should come back later. Maybe she should forget trying to talk to him at all—or at least choose a different venue for their conversation. The last time she'd been in his office with him was when the prince had kissed her.

Okay, it probably wasn't a good idea to think about that kiss right now. Except that since Wednesday night, she'd barely been able to think about anything else.

She realized that she couldn't hear him talking anymore, and knocked again, louder this time.

"Come in."

She pushed open the door and stepped inside.

He looked up, as if surprised to see her. He probably was. They'd both been tiptoeing around each other for the past several days.

"We never did finish the conversation we started to have about Riley," she reminded him.

"I assumed if there was cause for concern I would hear about it."

"Well, actually, I do have some concerns. Primarily about her eating habits."

"I have lunch and dinner with my daughter almost every day," he said. "Other than her preference for chicken nuggets, I haven't observed any problem."

"I wouldn't say it's a problem," she hedged. "At least not yet."

His brows lifted. "You came in here to talk about something that isn't yet a problem?"

She felt her cheeks flush. "Riley seems to eat a lot for such a young child, and she has dessert after lunch and dinner—every day."

"So?"

"If she continues to eat the way she does now, it won't be

long before she's battling weight and possibly even health issues."

"She's not even four."

She didn't disagree with what he was saying, and it wasn't Riley's weight that worried her. It was the pattern that she could see. She knew there was an easy fix for the problem, but only if the prince agreed to cooperate.

"She eats too much and exercises too little," she said bluntly.

"Should I hire a personal trainer for her?"

"No, Your Highness, you should stop hiring people and start spending time with her."

His brows lifted in silent challenge.

"I know I haven't been here very long," Hannah said. "But I've noticed that you don't interact with Riley very much outside of mealtimes."

"Then maybe you've also noticed that I have a lot of work to do and Riley is busy with her own lessons."

"Yes, I have noticed that, too," she admitted. "And I think that's why Riley is overeating."

"I'm not following."

She hesitated, torn between reluctance to disturb the status quo that obviously mattered to him and determination to open his eyes to some harsh truths. In the end, she decided his relationship with Riley was more important than anything else—her job included.

"The only time Riley sees you throughout the day is at lunch and dinner, so she does everything that she can to extend those mealtimes," she explained. "As soon as her plate is cleared away, you disappear, and I think that she's asking for second helpings so that you stay at the table with her. It's not because she's hungry, but because she's starving for your attention, Your Highness."

His gaze narrowed dangerously. "How dare you—"

"I dare," she interrupted, "because you entrusted Riley

into my care and I'm looking out for her best interests, Your Highness."

"Well, I don't believe it's in my daughter's best interests to put her on a diet."

She was horrified by the very thought. "That isn't what I'm suggesting at all."

"Then what are you suggesting?"

"That you rearrange your schedule to spend a few hours every day with Riley, somewhere other than the dining room."

"You can't be serious," he said, his tone dismissive. "And even if you are, she doesn't have that much time to spare any more than I do."

"Which is the other thing I wanted to talk to you about," she forged ahead before she lost her nerve.

"Go on," he urged, albeit with a decided lack of enthusiasm.

"A four-year-old needs time to play, Your Highness."

"Riley has plenty of time to play."

She shook her head. "She plays the piano, but she doesn't do anything else that a typical four-year-old does—anything just for fun. She paints with watercolors but doesn't know what to do with sidewalk chalk. She doesn't know how to jump rope or hit a shuttlecock, and she's never even kicked a soccer ball around."

"Because she isn't interested in any of those things."

"How do you know?" Hannah asked softly.

He frowned. "Because she's never asked to participate in those kinds of activities."

"Did she ask for piano lessons?"

"No," he admitted. "Not in so many words. But when she sat down and began to play, it was patently obvious that she had a talent that needed to be nurtured."

"And how do you know she's not a potential all-star soccer player if you don't give her the opportunity to try?"

"If she wants to kick a ball around, I have no objections," he said dismissively. "Now, if that's all—"

"No, it's not all," she interrupted. "There's the issue of her French lessons—"

"If there's any issue with her French lessons, you should discuss it with Monsieur Larouche."

"And I suppose I should direct all inquires about her Italian lessons to Signora Ricci and about her German lessons to Herr Weichelt?"

"You're starting to catch on."

She bristled at the sarcasm in his tone. "I thought we were past this already. Why are you acting like you don't care when I know that you do?"

"You're right," he agreed. "I do care—enough that I've hired qualified people to ensure she has everything she needs."

"When we talked the other night—" she felt her cheeks flush and prayed that he wouldn't notice "—you said that you were willing to make some changes. All I'm asking for is a couple of hours of your time every day."

He drummed his fingers on his desk, as if considering. Or maybe he was just impatient for her to finish.

"You said you wanted to get it right," she reminded him. "The only way to do that is to spend time with your daughter. To get to know her and let her get to know you, and that's not going to happen if you insist on keeping nannies and business obligations between you."

"It's the business that allows me to pay your salary," he pointed out to her.

"I'll gladly take a cut in my pay if you promise to give Riley at least two hours."

Once again, Hannah had surprised him. "I don't usually let my employees set the conditions of their employment."

"But this isn't a usual situation, is it?" she countered. "And I know you want what's best for Riley."

How could he possibly argue with that? And truthfully, he didn't want to. Although it was against his better judgment to give in to a woman whom he was beginning to suspect would try to take a mile for every inch he gave her, he wasn't opposed to her suggestion. After all, his time at Cielo del Norte was supposed to be something of a vacation from the daily demands of his company.

It's hardly a vacation if you're working all the time.

He heard Sam's words, her gently chiding tone, clearly in his mind.

It had been a familiar argument, and one that he'd always let her win—because it hadn't been a sacrifice to spend time with the wife that he'd loved more than anything in the world. But Sam was gone now, and without her a vacation held no real appeal. And yet he'd continued to spend his summers at the beach house because he knew that she would be disappointed if he abandoned the tradition. Just as he knew she'd be disappointed if he didn't accede to Hannah's request.

During Sam's pregnancy, they'd had long conversations about their respective childhoods and what they wanted for their own child. Sam had been adamant that their daughter would grow up in a home where she felt secure and loved. She didn't want Riley to be raised by a series of nannies, as he had been raised. Michael had agreed. He had few fond memories of his own childhood—and none after the death of his father—and he couldn't deny that he wanted something more, something better, for Riley. Except that without Sam to guide him, he didn't know what that something more and better could be.

Now Hannah was here, demanding that he spend time with his daughter, demanding that he be the father that Sam would want him to be. And he couldn't—didn't want to—turn away from that challenge. But he had to ask, "How do you know that spending more time with me is what Riley wants or needs?"

"Because you're her father and the only parent she has left," she said simply.

It was a fact of which he was well aware and the origin of all his doubts. He knew he was all Riley had—and he worried that he wasn't nearly enough. And he resented the nanny's determination to make him confront those fears. "Why is this so important to you?" he countered. "I mean, at the end of the summer, you'll walk away from both of us. Why do you care about my relationship with my daughter?"

He saw a flicker of something—sadness or maybe regret—in the depths of her stormy eyes before she glanced away. "Because I want something better for her than to get an email from you twenty years in the future telling her that she has a new stepmother," she finally responded.

Dios. He scrubbed his hands over his face. He'd forgotten that Hannah wasn't just Phillip Marotta's niece but that she'd lived with the doctor since coming to Tesoro del Mar as a child. Obviously there were some unresolved father-daughter issues in her background, and while those issues weren't any of his business, he knew that his relationship with his own daughter *was* his concern. And if Hannah was right about Riley's behavior, he had reason to be concerned.

"Okay," he agreed.

"Okay?" She seemed surprised by his acquiescence.

He nodded and was rewarded with a quick grin that lit up her whole face.

"I'd like to start this afternoon," she told him.

He glanced at his schedule, because it was a habit to do so before making any kind of commitment with respect to his time, and because he needed a reason to tear his gaze away from her mesmerizing smile. She truly was a beautiful woman, and he worried that spending more time with her along with his daughter would be as much torment as pleasure.

"If that works for you," Hannah said, as if she was expecting him to say that it didn't.

"That works just fine," he assured her.

She started for the door, paused with her hand on the knob. "Just one more thing."

"What's that?"

"When you're with Riley, the BlackBerry stays out of sight."

Chapter Nine

When Caridad told her that Monsieur Larouche had called to cancel his morning lesson with Riley, Hannah took it as a positive sign. Not for Monsieur Larouche, of course, and she sincerely hoped that the family emergency wasn't anything too serious, but she was grateful for the opportunity to get Riley outside and gauge her interest in something a little more physical than her usual activities.

Whether by accident or design, Karen had left a few of Grace's toys behind after their visit the previous week, including the little girl's soccer ball. And when Riley's piano lesson was finished, Hannah lured her outside with the promise of a surprise.

The princess looked from her nanny to the pink ball and back again. "What's the surprise?"

"I'm going to teach you how to play soccer."

"Soccer?" Riley wrinkled her nose.

"It's fun," she promised. "And very simple. Basically you

run around the field kicking a ball and trying to put it in the goal."

"I know what soccer is," the child informed her. "I've seen it on TV."

"It's not just on television—it's the most popular sport in the world."

"I don't play sports."

Hannah dropped the ball and when it bounced, she kicked it up to her thigh, then juggled it over to the other thigh, then back down to one foot and over to the other, before catching it again. "Why not?"

"Because I'm a princess," she said.

But Hannah noticed that she was looking at the ball with more curiosity than aversion now. "Oh—I didn't realize that you weren't allowed—"

"I'm allowed," Riley interrupted. "But I have more important things to do."

"Okay," Hannah agreed easily, slipping her foot under the ball and tossing it into the air.

"What does that mean?" the child demanded.

"I'm simply agreeing with you," she said, continuing to juggle the ball between her feet. "Playing soccer isn't important—it's just fun."

"And it's time for my French lesson anyway," the princess informed her, the slightest hint of wistfulness in her voice.

"You're not having a French lesson today."

"But it's Monday. I always have French after piano on Monday."

"Monsieur Larouche can't make it today."

Riley worried her bottom lip, uncomfortable with last-minute changes to her schedule.

"But if you'd rather study than learn to play soccer, you can go back inside and pull out your French books," Hannah assured her.

"Can you teach me how to do that?" Riley asked, mesmerized by the quick movements of the ball.

"I can try." She looked at the girl's pretty white dress and patent shoes. "But first we'd better change your clothes."

As Hannah scanned the contents of the child's closet, then rifled through the drawers of her dressers, she realized that dressing Riley appropriately for outdoor play was easier said than done.

"Who does your shopping?" she muttered.

"My aunt Marissa."

"It's as if she was expecting you to have tea with the queen every day." She looked at the shoes neatly shelved in three rows on the bottom of the closet. There were at least fifteen pairs in every shade from white to black but not a single pair without tassels or bows or flowers.

"Tesoro del Mar doesn't have a queen," the princess informed her primly. "It's a principality."

Hannah continued to survey the child's wardrobe. "Do you even own a T-shirt or shorts? Or sneakers?"

Riley shrugged.

"Well, I think before we get started, we need to find a mall."

"There's a bookstore at the mall," the little girl said, brightening.

"Shorts and shoes first," Hannah insisted. "Then we'll see."

"Maybe we could find a book about soccer," Riley suggested.

Hannah had to laugh. "You're pretty clever, aren't you?"

"That's what my teachers say."

"We'll go shopping after lunch," Hannah promised.

Though Michael didn't believe that Riley was starved for his attention as Hannah had claimed, he did make a point of paying close attention to her behavior at lunch. And he was dismayed to realize that the nanny was right. As soon as he had finished eating and she thought he might leave the table, she asked if she could have some more pasta salad. And after she finished her second helping of pasta salad, she asked for dessert.

"What did you want to do after lunch?" he asked her, while she was finishing up her pudding.

"I have quiet time until four o'clock and then…" The words faded away, and Riley frowned when she saw him shaking his head.

"I didn't ask what was on your schedule but what you wanted to do."

The furrow in her brow deepened, confirming that Hannah hadn't been so far off base after all. His daughter truly didn't know what to do if it wasn't penciled into her schedule.

"Because I was thinking maybe we could spend some time together."

Riley's eyes grew wide. "Really?"

He forced a smile, while guilt sliced like a knife through his heart. Had he really been so preoccupied and neglectful that his daughter was surprised by such a casual invitation?

"Really," he promised her.

"Well, Hannah said we could go shopping after lunch."

He looked at the nanny, his narrowed gaze clearly telegraphing his thoughts: *I agreed to your plan but I most definitely did not agree to shopping.*

"Your daughter has an impressive wardrobe that is completely devoid of shorts and T-shirts and running shoes," she explained.

"So make a list of what she needs and I'll send—"

One look at his daughter's dejected expression had him changing his mind.

With an inward sigh, he said, "Make a list so that we don't forget anything."

* * *

After two hours at the mall, with Rafe and two other guards forming a protective circle around the trio of shoppers, Michael noted that Hannah was almost as weary of shopping as he. But they had one more stop before they could head back to Cielo del Norte—the bookstore. He bought her a latte at the little café inside the store and they sat, surrounded by shopping bags, and discreetly flanked by guards, in the children's section while Riley—shadowed by Rafe—browsed through the shelves.

"We got a lot more than what was on the list."

"You said she didn't have anything," he reminded her.

"But she didn't need three pairs of running shoes."

Except that Riley had insisted that she did, showing how the different colors coordinated with the various outfits she'd chosen.

"She gets her fashion sense from my sister," he told her. "One day when we were visiting, Marissa spilled a drop of coffee on her shirt, so she went to find a clean one. But she didn't just change the shirt, she changed her shoes and her jewelry, too."

Hannah laughed. "I probably would have put on a sweater to cover up the stain."

"Sam was more like that," he admitted. "She didn't worry too much about anything. Except official royal appearances—then she would stress about every little detail like you wouldn't believe."

He frowned as he lifted his cup to his lips. He didn't often talk about Sam, not to other people. It was as if his memories were too precious too share—as if by revealing even one, he'd be giving up a little piece of her. And he wondered what it meant—if anything—that he found it so easy to talk to Hannah about Sam now. Was it just that he knew he could trust her to listen and not pass judgment, or was it a sign that he was finally starting to let go of the past and look to the future?

"Well, I should have realized that Riley's closet wouldn't be filled with all those frills and ruffles if it wasn't what she liked," Hannah commented now.

"You weren't into frills and ruffles as a child?"

"Never. And when I was Riley's age…" She paused, as if trying to remember. "My parents were missionaries, so we traveled a lot, and to a lot of places I probably don't even remember. But I think we were in Tanzania then, or maybe it was Ghana. In either case, I was more likely running naked with the native children than wearing anything with bows."

He tried to imagine her as a child, running as wild as she'd described. But his mind had stuck on the word *naked* and insisted on trying to picture her naked now. After having seen the delectable curves outlined by her bathing suit, it didn't take much prompting for his imagination to peel down the skinny straps of sleek fabric to reveal the fullness of creamy breasts tipped with rosy nipples that eagerly beaded in response to the brush of his fingertips. And when he dipped his head—

"Look, Daddy, I found a book about soccer."

Nothing like the presence of a man's almost-four-year-old daughter to effectively obliterate a sexual fantasy, Michael thought.

Then Riley climbed into his lap to show him the pictures, and he found that he didn't regret her interruption at all.

"That's an interesting book," he agreed.

"Can we buy it?"

He resisted the instinct to tell her yes, because he knew from experience that it wouldn't be the only book she wanted and he was trying to follow Hannah's advice to not give her everything she wanted.

"Let me think about it," he told her.

She considered that for a moment, and he braced himself

for the quivering lip and the shimmer of tears—or the hands on the hips and the angry scowl—but she just nodded. "Can you hold on to it while I keep looking?"

"I'll keep it right beside me," he promised.

Hannah watched the little girl skip back to the stacks. "She's so thrilled that you're here," she told him.

"I guess I didn't realize that it took so little to make her happy," he admitted.

"We've already been here longer than the two hours I asked for."

"I'm not counting the minutes," he assured her. "Besides, I'm enjoying this, too."

"Really?"

He chuckled at the obvious skepticism in her tone. "Let's just say, the shopping part wasn't as bad as I'd feared. And this part—" he lifted his cup "—is a definite pleasure."

"You better be careful," she warned. "Or you just might live up to that potential I was talking about."

He took another sip of his coffee before asking the question that had been hovering at the back of his mind. "Was your father so neglectful?"

"How did my father come into this?" she countered.

But the casual tone of her reply was too deliberate, and he knew that beneath the lightly spoken words was buried a world of hurt.

"I think he's always been there, I just didn't realize it before."

"It's true that my father and I aren't close," she admitted.

"Because he never had enough time for you," he guessed.

"He never had *any* time for me." She cupped her hands around her mug and stared into it, as if fascinated by the ring of foam inside. "I'm not even sure that he ever wanted to be a father," she finally continued, "but my mom wanted a baby and there was no doubt that he loved my mom, and I thought it was enough to know that my mom loved me."

"Until she died," he guessed.

"But then I had my uncle Phillip. He pretty much raised me after she was gone."

"I have to say, he did a pretty good job."

She smiled at that. "He was a wonderful example of what a father should be—of the kind of father I know *you* can be."

He hoped—for Riley's sake even more than his own—that he wouldn't disappoint her.

Despite the new outfit and the proper shoes, it didn't take Hannah long to realize that Riley was never going to be an all-star soccer player. It wasn't just that the child seemed to lack any kind of foot-eye coordination, but that she quickly grew discouraged by her own ineptitude. The more patient and understanding Hannah tried to be, the more discouraged Riley seemed to get.

So after a few days on the lawn with little progress and a lot of frustration, she took Riley into town again so that the little girl could decide what she wanted to try next. The sporting goods store had an extensive selection of everything, and Hannah and Riley—and Rafe—wandered up and down several aisles before they found the racquet sports section.

"I want to play tennis," Riley announced.

Since there was a court on the property, Hannah hoped it might be a better choice for the princess, who immediately gravitated toward a racquet with a pink handle and flowers painted on the frame.

Now she had a half-full bucket of tennis balls beside her with the other half scattered around the court. She'd been tossing them to Riley so that she could hit them with her racquet, with very little success. The child had connected once, and she'd been so startled when the ball made contact with the webbing that the racquet had slipped right out of her hand. But she'd scooped it up again and refocused, her big brown eyes narrowed with determination. Unfortunately, it seemed that the harder she tried, the wider she missed.

The prince would happily have paid for a professional instructor, but Hannah wanted to keep the lessons fun for Riley by teaching the little girl herself. But after only half an hour, neither of them was having very much fun. The more balls that Riley missed the more frustrated she got, and the more frustrated she got the less she was able to focus on the balls coming toward her.

"She needs to shorten her grip."

Hannah looked up to see a handsome teenager standing at the fence, watching them with an easy smile on his face.

"She needs a better teacher," she admitted.

"Kevin!" Riley beamed at him. "I'm going to learn to play tennis just like you."

The boy's brows lifted. "Just like me, huh?"

She nodded. "Hannah's teaching me."

"Trying to, anyway." She offered her hand. "Hannah Castillo."

"Kevin Fuentes," he said.

"Caridad and Estavan's son," she suddenly realized. "I've seen you helping out your dad around the yard." And she'd heard him in the kitchen, arguing with his mother, though she didn't share that information. "So you play tennis?" she queried.

"Every chance I get."

"Caridad says that Kevin's going to get a scholarship," Riley informed her. "But only if he pays attention in class and forgets the pretty girls."

Hannah couldn't help but laugh as the boy's cheeks flushed.

"You have an awfully big mouth for such a little kid," Kevin said, but the reprimand was tempered with a wry smile as he ruffled Riley's hair.

The little kid in question beamed up at him in obvious adoration.

"Do you want me to show her how to adjust her grip?" Kevin asked.

"I'd be extremely grateful," Hannah assured him.

The teenager dropped to his knees on the court beside her.

"I'm going to play just like you," the little girl said again.

"It took me a lot of years of practice." Even as he spoke, he adjusted the position of Riley's grip on the handle of her racquet.

"I'm a fast learner," she assured him.

"You need to learn to be patient," he told her, guiding her arm in a slow-motion demonstration of a ground stroke. "And to let the ball come to you."

He nodded toward Hannah, signaling her to toss a ball.

As soon as the ball left her hand, Riley was trying to reach for it, but Kevin held her back, waiting then guiding her arm to meet the ball.

The fuzzy yellow ball hit the center of the webbing with a soft *thwop,* and Hannah had to duck to avoid being hit by its return. Riley turned to Kevin, her eyes almost as wide as her smile. "I did it."

"You did," he agreed. "Now let's see if you can do it again."

After a few more easy tosses and careful returns, Riley said, "I want to hit it harder."

"You should work on accuracy before power," Kevin told her.

Riley pouted but continued to practice the slow, steady stroke he'd shown her.

"You're a lot better at this than I am," Hannah said, tossing another ball.

He gave a half shrug. "This comes easily to me. Trying

to figure out what Hamlet's actually saying in his infamous 'to be or not to be' speech doesn't."

"It's really not that complicated, although the language of the time can make it seem so," she said, not wanting to delve into the details of the tragic hero's contemplations about suicide in front of a four-year-old.

"And my teacher talks like he was born in Shakespeare's time."

"It can't be that bad," Hannah protested, tossing the last ball.

"It's worse," he insisted. "I have an essay due tomorrow in which I have to decide—in a thousand words—whether or not Hamlet really did love Ophelia."

She couldn't help but smile, thinking that—like most teenage boys—he'd much rather talk about the character's thirst for revenge than any of his more tender emotions. But all she said was, "*Hamlet* has always been one of my favorite plays."

He turned to look at her now, his expression a combination of surprise and disbelief. "Really?"

She shrugged, almost apologetically. "I like Shakespeare."

"Can we do some more?" Riley interrupted to demand.

"First lessons should be short," Kevin told her. "And the lesson's not over until you put all of the balls back in the bucket."

If Hannah had been the one to ask Riley to retrieve the scattered balls, she had no doubt the princess would have refused. But when Kevin spoke, the little girl happily trotted off to do his bidding.

"You're really good with her," Hannah noted.

"She's a good kid."

"Would you be willing to work with her on some other tennis basics some time?"

"Sure," he agreed readily. "It's not like I'm doing much of anything else these days, aside from summer school."

"Speaking of which," she said. "Why don't you bring your essay up to the main house tonight?"

His eyes lit up. "Are you going to fix it for me?"

She laughed. "You're assuming it needs fixing."

"It does," he assured her.

"Then we'll fix it together."

Friday morning after breakfast, Hannah and Riley were working on a jigsaw puzzle in the library when Caridad came in to water the plants. She looked from the little girl to the clock then back again and frowned.

"Signora Ricci is late today," she noted.

"Signora Ricci isn't coming today," Hannah told her.

The housekeeper held a towel beneath the spout of the watering can to ensure it didn't drip as she moved from one planter to the next. "Is she ill?"

"No, she's on vacation."

"She would not have gone on vacation without first arranging a replacement and certainly not without discussing the matter with the prince." The implication being that the prince would then have told her, which of course he would have—if he'd known.

"The vacation was my idea," Hannah admitted. "And more for the benefit of the princess than her teacher."

"You have talked to Prince Michael about this?" the housekeeper prompted.

"I tried, but the prince assured me that any concerns about his daughter's language instruction were best discussed with her instructor."

"I had my doubts," the housekeeper admitted, "when the prince first hired you. But now I think that maybe he knew what he was doing."

"Even if he would disagree?"

Caridad smiled. "Especially if he would disagree."

She finished watering the rest of the plants before she

spoke again. "Kevin said you're helping him with his Shake-speare essay."

"In exchange for him helping Riley learn to play tennis," Hannah explained, remembering their earlier conversation in which the housekeeper had expressed reluctance to accept help for her son without some kind of payment in return.

The housekeeper waved the towel in her hand, obviously satisfied by the exchange of services. "I have no objections," she said. "If you are half as good a teacher as you are a nanny, he will write a good paper."

Only a few weeks earlier, Hannah hadn't been certain that she even wanted to be a nanny, but in all of her years of teaching, she'd never received a compliment that meant as much to her as Caridad's.

Chapter Ten

There were still occasions when Michael had to return to Port Augustine for meetings with clients, but he rarely stayed away overnight. Unfortunately, today's meeting had stretched out longer than he'd anticipated because the client refused to be satisfied with any of the advertisement proposals presented to her.

Michael believed strongly in customer satisfaction, so he suggested that they continue their discussions over dinner. He'd learned that a less formal atmosphere often facilitated a more open exchange of information, but as they shared tapas and wine, he quickly realized that the client had chosen RAM less for the needs of her company and more for her personal interest in him.

He knew that he should be flattered, but truthfully he was growing tired of deflecting unwanted advances. Especially when he'd given her no indication that he was interested in anything more than a business relationship. But as he drove back to Cielo del Norte, he found himself wondering what was wrong with him that he wasn't attracted to an obviously attractive woman. A few weeks ago, he could have argued that he just wasn't ready, that he couldn't imagine himself with anyone who wasn't Sam.

Since Hannah had moved into Cielo del Norte, he'd realized that was no longer true. So why couldn't he be attracted to someone other than Hannah? What was it about his daughter's temporary nanny that had got under his skin?

As a result of his unproductive dinner meeting, he returned to the beach house much later than he'd intended. Not only had he missed hanging out with his daughter during the day, but he was too late to tuck her into bed, as had become their nightly ritual. When he went upstairs to check on her, he found that she was sleeping peacefully with Sara tucked under her arm. He brushed a light kiss on her forehead and her lips curved, just a little, in response to the touch.

He went back downstairs, thinking that he would pour a glass of his favorite cabernet and sit out under the stars for a while. When he approached the kitchen, he heard the sounds of conversation. The soft, smoky tone was definitely Hannah's; the deeper, masculine voice wasn't as familiar.

It occurred to him then that she'd given up her whole life to spend the summer at Cielo del Norte, and in the first month that she'd been in residence, she hadn't asked for any time off to go out. He knew that her friend Karen had visited a few times with her children, because Riley would tell him all about her "best friend" Grace and describe in great detail everything that they'd done together. But it was Hannah's visitor who was on his mind now.

Was the man in the kitchen an old friend? Maybe even a boyfriend? He frowned at the thought. His frown deepened when it occurred to him that there had been no other vehicles in the drive when he'd pulled in.

He paused in the doorway, shamelessly eavesdropping.

"Pay close attention to the characters of both Marlow and

Kurtz," Hannah was saying now. "And which one seems, to you, to be the real hero of the book."

It didn't sound like date conversation to him. On the other hand, he hadn't been on a date in more than sixteen years, so what did he know?

"But can't there be—"

Her guest looked up as he walked into the room, and the boy—Caridad's son, Michael realized with a sense of relief—pushed his chair away from the table to execute an awkward bow. "Your Highness."

He waved Kevin back to his seat. "I didn't realize you were…entertaining," he said to Hannah.

"I didn't realize you were home," she countered.

He noted the books that were open on the table, surrounded by scraps of paper with notes scribbled on them.

"We're working on the outline for Kevin's next assignment," she explained.

Michael surveyed the assortment of bottles in the wine rack, automatically reached for a familiar label. Maybe she did believe she was helping the boy study, but it was obvious to him that Hannah's student was more interested in her than in anything she was trying to explain to him.

"I thought school was out for the summer," he commented.

"For most people," Kevin said. "But my mom decided to torture me with summer school—as if spending ten months in the classroom wasn't already torture enough."

Hannah smiled as she gathered together the loose papers and inserted them into a folder. "Look on the bright side— if you get your credit this summer, you won't have to take another English course until college."

"That's still too soon for me," the boy grumbled.

"I want to see your draft outline by Wednesday," Hannah told him.

"I'll have it ready," he promised. Then he bowed again. "Good evening, Your Highness."

"Good evening, Kevin." He uncorked the bottle of wine. "So how long have you been tutoring my housekeeper's son?"

"It isn't a formal arrangement," she said. "And it doesn't interfere in any way with my taking care of Riley."

"I'm not worried—just curious as to how this arrangement came about, and whether Caridad knows that her son has a major crush on you."

"It came about because Kevin's been helping Riley with her ground stroke, and Caridad knows that his infatuation will be over before he signs his name to his final exam."

"How can she be so sure?"

"Teenage boys are notoriously fickle."

"That's probably true enough," he acknowledged, even as he mentally berated himself for being no less fascinated by the sexy curves outlined by her T-shirt than the teenage boy who had just left.

And no doubt he would have shown more interest in English Lit when he was in school if he'd had a teacher like Hannah Castillo. But all of the teachers at the exclusive prep school he'd attended had been male and seemingly as old as the institution itself.

She finished packing away her notes, then pushed away from the table. "I'm going to go check on Riley."

"I just did." He took two glasses out of the cupboard. "She's sleeping."

"Oh. Okay."

"Come on," he said, heading toward the sliding French doors that led out to the terrace. He bypassed the chairs to sit at the top of the steps, where he could see the moon reflecting on the water.

Hannah had paused just outside the doors, as if reluctant to come any closer. "It's late."

"It's not that late," he chided, pouring the wine. "And it's a beautiful night."

She ventured closer and accepted the glass he offered before lowering herself onto the step beside him. "How was your meeting?"

"I don't want to talk about the meeting." He tipped his glass to his lips, sipped. He didn't even want to think about the time he'd wasted, time he would much have preferred to spend with his daughter—and her nanny. "How did things go with Riley today?"

"I think we're making some real progress."

"I know she's enjoying the tennis lessons," he admitted.

Hannah smiled. "That's more because of Kevin than the game, I think."

He frowned. "Are you telling me that my daughter has a crush on the boy who has a crush on her nanny?"

"It's a distinct possibility," she told him. "At least the part about Riley's feelings for Kevin."

"I should have my brother talk to the Minister of the Environment about testing the water out here," he muttered.

She smiled again. "She's a little girl and he's a good-looking boy who pays her a lot of attention."

"You think he's good-looking?"

"That was hardly the most relevant part of my statement," she said dryly.

"Maybe not," he acknowledged. "But he's also seventeen years old."

"Relax, I don't think she's planning the wedding just yet," she teased.

"I was making the point of his age to you," Michael admitted.

"I know—oh!" She grabbed his arm and pointed. "Look."

Her eyes were wide with wonder as she stared up at the sky, but it was the press of her breast against his arm that snagged his attention.

"I've never seen a shooting star before," she told him.

She was still holding on to his arm, though he wasn't sure if she was conscious of that fact. And while he couldn't deny the quick jolt of lust that went through him, he realized that there was something deeper beneath the surface. A sense of happiness and contentment that came from just sitting here with Hannah. A sense of happiness and contentment that he hadn't felt in a very long time.

"It was right here on this terrace with my dad that I saw my first-ever shooting star," he told her.

She seemed surprised by the revelation, and he realized that she probably was. Over the past couple of weeks, they'd spent a lot of time together and engaged in numerous conversations, but either Riley was with them or was the center of those discussions. He certainly wasn't in the habit of sharing personal details of his own life.

"Did you spend a lot of time here as a kid?" she asked him now.

"Yeah. Although not as much after my dad passed away."

"It was probably hard for your mom, to return to a place with so many memories."

While he appreciated the sympathy in her tone, he knew that her compassion—in this instance—was misplaced. "It wasn't the memories she had trouble with, it was the lack of exclusive boutiques and five-star restaurants."

Hannah seemed puzzled by that.

"Do you know much about my family?" he asked.

"I know that your mother is the princess royal."

"And my father was a farmer."

"I didn't know that," she admitted.

"She claimed that she loved who he was, and then she spent the next fifteen years trying to change him into someone else. Someone better suited to her station."

She didn't prompt him for more information or pry for details, and maybe that was why he found it easy to talk to her. Why he found himself telling her things that he'd never told anyone else before.

"After my dad died, she changed her focus to my brother and I. She had such big plans and ambitions for us."

"I would think she'd be very proud of both of you."

His smile was wry. "She refers to RAM as my 'little company' and despairs that I will ever do anything worthwhile. And even Cameron's position in the prince regent's cabinet isn't good enough, because she wanted him sitting on the throne."

"What were her plans for Marissa?" she asked curiously.

"Lucky for her, my baby sister pretty much flies under Elena's radar."

"How does she manage that?"

"She's female."

Hannah's brows lifted.

"I'm not saying it's right—just that it is what it is. Even though the Tesorian laws were recently changed to ensure equal titles and property would be inherited regardless of gender, she's always believed that it's the men who hold the power.

"I remember how thrilled she was to find out that Sam was expecting—and how disappointed she was when she learned that we were having a daughter. She didn't even pretend otherwise."

"But Riley is such a wonderful little girl," she protested.

"And my mother barely knows her," he admitted. "She's the only grandparent my daughter has, and she doesn't even make an effort to spend time with her."

Not only did Elena not spend time with Riley, the princess royal had suggested sending his little girl away to boarding school, the mere idea of which still made Michael's blood boil.

"She's lucky, then, to have a father who's making such an effort to be part of her life," Hannah told him.

"I missed her today," he admitted, pushing all thoughts of his mother aside. "And I hated not being here to tuck her in."

"She was disappointed, but thrilled when you called from the restaurant to say good-night."

"She said you had a picnic on the beach at lunch."

"I thought it might take her mind off of the fact that you weren't here."

"She sounded as if she really enjoyed it," he said.

Hannah smiled. "She got a bit of a surprise when she threw the crusts of her sandwich away and the gulls swooped in to take them."

"Was she scared?"

"She did shriek at first, but then she was okay. She's already decided that she's keeping the crusts of her toast from breakfast tomorrow so that she can feed them again."

"Then we'll have to make sure we have toast for breakfast," he agreed.

And that was how they ended up on the dock the next morning. Except Hannah noticed that while she and Riley were tossing bread to the birds, the prince had wandered farther back on the dock. After the little girl had tossed the last few pieces to the hungry gulls, Hannah took Riley's hand and guided her back to where her father was standing, with his back to the water and his BlackBerry to his ear.

She put her hands on her hips. "What do you think you're doing?"

Michael stopped in midsentence. "I'm just—"

Before he could finish speaking, she'd grabbed the phone from his hand.

"We had a deal," she reminded him.

And he'd stuck to the deal, which had been a pleasant surprise to Hannah. At least until now. In fact, he'd been so diligent about following the rules that she was prepared to cut him some slack—after she'd made him feel just a little bit guilty.

"I know, but—"

"No phones, Daddy." It was Riley who interrupted his explanation this time, and before he could say anything further, she took the phone from Hannah and flung it over her shoulder.

Hannah gasped as Michael's head whipped around, his gaze following the instrument as it sailed through the air, seeming to tumble end over end in slow motion before it splashed into the ocean.

She knew that Riley had acted on impulse, without any thought about what she was doing or the potential consequences, and that the prince was going to be furious. The only possible way to do damage control was to get Riley to apologize immediately and sincerely. But when Hannah opened her mouth to speak to the little girl, the only sound that came out was a muffled laugh.

"I was in the middle of a conversation with the vice president of a major telecommunications company," the prince informed her.

"You'll have to tell him that your call—" she tried to muffle her chuckle with a cough "—got dropped."

He glowered at her.

"I'm sorry. I know it's not funny…" But she couldn't finish, because she was laughing.

"If you know it's not funny, why are you laughing?" he demanded.

Riley looked from one to the other, measuring her father's stern visage against her nanny's amusement, as if trying to figure out how much trouble she was in.

"I don't know," Hannah admitted. "But I can't seem to stop."

"She threw my BlackBerry into the ocean."

She was turning red from holding her breath, trying to hold in the chuckles.

His eyes narrowed. "You really *do* think it's funny, don't you?"

She shook her head, wanting to deny it. But her efforts were futile.

"Well, then," Michael said. "Let's see if you think this is funny."

She fell silent when he scooped her into his arms, suddenly unable to remember why she'd been laughing. The sensation of being held close in his arms blocked everything else out. Everything but the heat and hardness of his body— the strong arms holding on to her, one at her back and one under her knees; the firm muscles of his chest beneath her cheek. She was tempted to rub her cheek against him and purr like a kitten, inhaling the enticingly spicy scent of the furiously sexy man. Oh, if only he would hold her like this forever—

The thought had barely formed in her mind when she realized that he was no longer holding on to her at all. Instead, she was flying through the air.

The shock of that had barely registered before she hit the water.

She came up dripping and sputtering, obviously as surprised as he had been when Riley had tossed his phone in the water, then she resolutely began to swim back to the dock. Any sense of satisfaction Michael had felt when he sent her on the same journey was gone. In fact, looking at her now as she pulled herself up onto the ladder, he was feeling distinctly unsatisfied. And very aroused.

He stared. He knew it was impolite, but he couldn't help himself. She usually dressed conservatively, keeping her feminine attributes well hidden. But now, with her pale pink T-shirt and white shorts soaked through and plastered to her body, there was no disguising the delicious curves she had tried to hide—or the sexy lace bra that covered her pert, round breasts but couldn't conceal the tight buds of her nipples.

He swallowed, hard.

She was at the top of the ladder now, and he offered his hand to help her up the last step.

She eyed him warily for a moment before she accepted.

Her hand was cool, but the touch heated his blood, and he realized that he was in serious trouble with this woman. Because even now, when he should be angry and amazed, he couldn't deny the attraction between them. An attraction that continued to grow stronger with each passing day.

"All in all, I'd say you fared better than my phone," he noted, trying to maintain some equilibrium.

She shoved a handful of sopping hair over her shoulder and, with obvious skepticism, asked, "How do you figure?"

"Your circuits aren't fried." As his were—or at least in serious danger of doing so.

"Are you going to throw me in the water, too, Daddy?" Riley looked at him with an expression that was half hopeful and half fearful.

"I might," he said, scooping her off of her feet and into his arms.

Riley shrieked and wrapped her arms tight around his neck. "No, Daddy, no."

"But you did a bad thing, throwing my phone into the water," he reminded her. "So there should be some kind of punishment."

She nodded her head, still clinging to him.

"What do you think that punishment should be?"

His daughter wrinkled her nose, as if seriously contemplating an answer to his question, then offered her suggestion. "Maybe no broccoli for me for a month?"

It was all he could do not to laugh himself—because he

knew how much she hated broccoli. "Nice try, Princess, but I think the punishment needs to be a little more immediate than that and more directly linked to the crime."

"An apology?" she suggested. "Because I am very sorry, Daddy."

"That's a good start, but not very convincing."

"Very, very sorry," she said, framing his face in her hands and kissing first one cheek and then the other.

"Much more convincing," he said.

She smiled at him, and it was the kind of smile he hadn't seen on her face in a very long time—a smile full of such pure joy that it actually made his heart ache.

He glanced over her head at Hannah, hoping to telegraph his appreciation to her because he knew that she was responsible for so many changes he'd seen in his daughter in the past few weeks. She was watching them and smiling, too, and he saw that there were tears in her eyes.

Since her first day at Cielo del Norte, Hannah had witnessed more and more examples of the strengthening bond between father and daughter. They'd come a long way in a short while, she realized. From virtual strangers who shared polite conversation across the dinner table to a father and daughter who genuinely enjoyed spending time together.

Watching them together filled her heart with happiness—and more than a little envy. Because as much as she wanted to believe that she'd played a part in bringing them together, her role had been peripheral. She was the outsider, as she'd been the outsider through most of her life.

Even when her uncle Phillip had brought her back to Tesoro del Mar, she'd been conscious of the fact that she didn't really belong. All she'd ever wanted was a home and a family of her own, a place where she was truly wanted and needed. But she'd be a fool to think she could find it here—even for a short while.

But there were moments—rare and precious moments that she knew she would hold in her heart forever—when she truly felt as if she was part of their world. Like when Riley reached for her hand as they walked on the beach. Or when the little girl spontaneously reached up to hug Hannah as she tucked her into bed at night.

She'd known from the beginning that her time with Riley and the prince wouldn't ever be anything more than temporary, but that knowledge hadn't stopped her from falling for the princess. There was simply no way she could have resisted a child who needed so much and somehow gave back so much more.

No, it didn't surprise her at all that the little girl had completely taken hold of her heart. The bigger surprise—and much bigger worry—was that she was very close to falling in love with the princess's father, too.

Chapter Eleven

It was the sound of Riley's screams that had Michael bolting out of his office a few days later. The screams were coming from the tennis courts, and he raced in that direction. Caridad, also summoned by the sound of the little girl's calls, was right behind him.

"Help! Daddy! Help!"

He would have been the first to admit that his daughter had a tendency to melodrama and that she did everything at full volume. But he'd learned to tell from the tone of her cries whether she was sad or frustrated or hurt, and he'd learned to distinguish between playful and fearful shouts. But he'd never heard her scream like this, and the sound chilled him to the bone.

"Someone! Please! Quick!"

As soon as she saw him, her screams turned to sobs. "Daddy, Daddy, you have to help."

He dropped to his knees beside her. "What happened? Where are you hurt?" He ran his hands over her as he spoke, his heart in his throat as he tried to determine the nature of her injury. The way she'd been screaming, he'd sincerely feared that she'd lost a limb or at least broken a bone. But aside from the red face streaked with tears, she appeared to be unharmed, and relief flooded through him like a wave.

"It's n-not m-me," she sobbed. "It's H-han-nah."

By this time, the housekeeper had caught up to them, and he saw that she had gone directly to where Hannah was kneeling on the court. Though the nanny had a hand to her head, she didn't seem to be in any dire straits.

With Riley clinging to his side, he ventured closer.

"I'm fine," he heard her saying, trying to shake Caridad off as she helped her to her feet.

But the older woman was resolute, and as she steered Hannah toward one of the benches along the sidelines of the court, he finally noticed the blood.

He halted abruptly, his stomach clenching.

"I d-didn't m-mean to d-do it," Riley managed between sobs. "It w-was an accid-dent."

He squeezed her gently, trying to reassure her but unable to tear his own gaze away from the crimson blood dripping down the side of Hannah's face.

"You are not fine," Caridad said to Hannah. "And you need to sit down while I get a towel and the antiseptic cream."

He'd yet to meet anyone who could ignore a direct order from the housekeeper when she spoke in that tone, and Hannah was no exception. She sat where Caridad directed.

"Come on, Riley," the housekeeper said. "You can help me find what we need."

Michael knew that Caridad didn't really need Riley's assistance but was trying to distract her from the situation. And Riley was eager to help, obediently falling into step behind the housekeeper. Michael moved over to the bench to check on Hannah.

"I guess that will teach me to walk up behind a little girl with a tennis racquet," she said ruefully.

"Is that what happened?" He kept his tone light, not wanting her to know how badly his insides were shaking. He guessed that she'd been cut right above the eye, because that's where she seemed to be applying pressure, but he couldn't tell for sure.

Hannah managed a smile. "Your daughter has a good set of lungs on her."

"That she does," he agreed.

"I'm sorry about the panic. I was trying to calm her down, but she saw the blood and then just started screaming."

Riley raced over with a neatly folded towel. "This one's for your head," she said, handing one to Hannah. "You're supposed to put pressure on the cut to stop the bleeding. Caridad's bringing the rest of the stuff."

The rest of the stuff turned out to be a washcloth and a basin of warm water, which she used to clean the blood off of the area around the cut, and a first-aid kit, from which she took an antiseptic wipe to dab gently against the wound. Then she instructed Hannah to keep the pressure on and went back inside to finish getting dinner ready.

"There's a lot of blood, Daddy." Riley spoke in an awed whisper.

"Head wounds always bleed a lot," Hannah said, trying to reassure her. "I'll put a Band-Aid on in a few minutes and—"

The prince laid his hand over hers, forcing her to lift the towel so that he could take another look at the gash. The blood immediately began to flow again. "I'm pretty sure it needs more than a Band-Aid."

"I'm sure it doesn't," she insisted.

"You're not a doctor," he reminded her.

"No, but I grew up with one, and he—"

"And he would want you to have this checked out," the prince said firmly.

As it turned out, her uncle Phillip had been at a day conference in San Pedro, so he arrived at Cielo del Norte within an hour of the housekeeper's call. By that time, the bleeding had mostly stopped and Hannah was lying down on a sofa in the library, reading.

Riley was sitting with her, keeping her company while she waited for the doctor to arrive. Despite her repeated assurances that she was okay, the child insisted on staying by her side.

"You only had to call and I would have come to visit," her uncle chided from the doorway. "You didn't need to create all this drama to get me out here."

"I'm having second thoughts about it now," she told him, easing herself back up to sitting position.

"Hi, Doctor Phil," Riley said.

He smiled at the nickname and offered the little girl a lollipop that he took out of his bag. "For after dinner."

She nodded and tucked it into the pocket of her shorts.

Phillip sat down beside his niece. "So how did this happen?"

"I hit Hannah with my racquet," Riley confessed.

"Forehand or backhand?" the doctor asked.

Riley had to think for a minute before answering that one. "Backhand."

"You must have a pretty powerful swing."

"I've been practicing lots," she admitted, sounding torn between pride and regret.

"Okay, let's see what kind of damage you did," he said, moving to examine the wound.

Hannah winced when he tipped her head back.

"Headache?" he asked, all teasing forgotten.

She nodded slowly.

"I'll give you something for that after I stitch this up."

He offered to let Riley stay to watch while he fixed up the wound. The little girl had seemed enthused about the prospect, but as soon as the needle pierced through the skin the first time, she disappeared quickly enough.

"Are you enjoying your job here?" Phillip asked Hannah when Riley had gone.

"Other than today, you mean?"

"Other than today," he agreed with a smile.

"I am," she said. "There was a period of adjustment— for all of us—but I think we've come a long way in a few weeks."

"The young princess seems very taken with you."

"I think she's feeling guilty."

"That could be part of it," he admitted.

Hannah sat patiently while he tied off the sutures, thinking about the little girl.

"I still miss my mom sometimes," she finally admitted.

If her uncle thought it was a strange statement, or one that came from out of nowhere, he gave no indication of it. Instead, he said, "I do, too."

"But I have a lot of memories of the time we spent together. Good memories."

"And Riley has none of her mother," he noted, following her train of thought.

"Do you think that makes it harder for her—because she doesn't have any memories to hold on to?"

"I'm sure there are times when she's conscious of a void in her life, but she seems pretty well-adjusted to me."

"How long do you think someone usually grieves?"

He taped a square of gauze over the sutures. "I'm not sure there's an answer to that question. Each relationship is different, therefore each grieving process is different."

She thought about her father's latest email again—and her

own surprise and anger when she read his note. "I thought my dad would love my mom forever."

"I'm sure he will," her uncle said gently. "But that doesn't mean he couldn't—or shouldn't—fall in love again."

She nodded, but her thoughts were no longer on her parents' relationship or her father's remarriage. "Do you think Prince Michael could fall in love again?"

"I'm sure he could," he said with a slight furrow in his brow. "But I wouldn't want to speculate on when that might happen, and I don't want you to forget that this is only a summer job."

"Don't worry—I have no desire to give up teaching to be a full-time nanny," she assured him.

"That's not what I meant."

"What did you mean?"

"I know you had a crush on the prince when you were younger, and I'm worried that being here may have rekindled those feelings."

"I did have a crush," she admitted. "But it was a childhood infatuation. I didn't know him then, and I didn't even like him when I first came here—he was so distant and reserved."

"And now you've fallen in love with him," he guessed.

She shook her head. "No. I have feelings for him—" deeper feelings than she was ready to admit even to herself "—but I'm smart enough to know that falling in love with a prince could never lead to anything but heartache."

"You're not nearly as smart as you think if you honestly believe that you can control what is in your heart," he warned her.

As Phillip finished packing up his bag, Caridad came in to invite him to stay for dinner. He declined the offer politely, insisting that he wanted to get on his way.

Hannah was sorry to see him go—she had missed him over the past several weeks, but she was also relieved by his

departure. Apparently he had shrewder observation skills
than she would have guessed, and she was very much afraid
he was right. And if she was falling in love with the prince,
she didn't want her uncle to be a witness to her folly.

Because she knew that it would be foolish to give her
heart to a man who could never love her back because he
was still in love with his wife. And she feared that her uncle
was right—that loving the prince might not be a matter of
choice, and that she already did.

After dinner, Hannah joined the prince and his daughter
in the media room to watch a movie. Riley insisted on sitting
between them with the bowl of popcorn in her lap, and while
the action on the screen kept her riveted for nearly ninety
minutes, she did sneak periodic glances at the bandage on
Hannah's head to ensure that it wasn't bleeding again.

"Bedtime," the prince told his daughter when the credits
began to roll.

"I can't go to bed," she protested. "I have to stay up in
case Hannah has a concuss."

"It's *concussion*," Hannah said. "And I don't."

"But what if you do?"

"Doctor Phil checked me over very thoroughly."

"But the medical book says you should be 'specially
vigi—" She wrinkled her nose, trying to remember the word.

"Vigilant?" her father suggested.

She nodded. "You should be 'specially vigilant when
someone gets hit in the head."

So that was what she'd been doing while Phillip stitched
up Hannah's wound—reading up on head injuries.

"I appreciate your concern," she told the little girl. "But
I'm really okay—I promise."

"You're not going to die?" The little girl's eyes were wide,
her tone worried.

"Not today."

"Does it hurt very much?" The child didn't sound worried so much as curious now.

"Not very much," she said, and it was true now that the acetaminophen her uncle had given her was finally starting to take the edge off of the pain.

"Do you want me to kiss it better?"

Hannah was as surprised as she was touched by the offer. "I think that would make it much better."

Riley leaned forward and very carefully touched her lips to the square of white gauze that had been taped over the wound.

"Okay?"

She nodded.

"You have to kiss it, too, Daddy."

Hannah's panicked gaze met with the prince's amused one.

"It's really much better now," she said to Riley.

"But if one kiss helps, then two should help twice as much," the little girl said logically.

"You can't argue with that," Michael told her.

"I guess not," she agreed.

"Kiss her, Daddy."

So he did. He leaned down and touched his lips gently to her forehead, just above the bandage. It was nothing more than a fleeting touch, barely more than a brush against her skin, but it made everything inside of her melt. Oh yeah, she was definitely falling.

He pulled back, looking into her eyes again. All traces of amusement were gone from his expression now, replaced by an intense awareness that rocked her to her very soul.

"Is that twice as much better?" Riley wanted to know.

Hannah forced a smile. "Twice as much."

"Now that Hannah's boo-boo has been kissed all better, it's bedtime for you," Michael reminded his daughter.

"Will you take me up, Daddy?"

"You bet," he said, and swept her off of her feet and into his arms.

Hannah let out an unsteady breath as they disappeared through the doorway. She felt the tiniest twinge of guilt knowing that she'd lied to the little girl. Because the truth was that the prince's kiss hadn't made anything better, it had only made her desire for him that much harder to ignore.

When Riley was all snug under her covers, Michael kissed her good-night and went back downstairs to find Hannah. He wasn't happy when he found her in the kitchen.

"You're supposed to be resting," he admonished.

"I'm not on my hands and knees scrubbing the floor—I'm just putting a couple of glasses in the dishwasher."

"Nevertheless—" He took her arm and steered her out of the room. "I don't want your uncle mad at me because you weren't following his orders."

"I can't imagine he would hold you responsible."

"And Riley is very concerned about you, too," he reminded her.

She smiled at that. "If I'd known a little cut above my eye would change her attitude toward me, I'd have let her take a swing at me weeks ago."

"I'm not sure that's a strategy I would actually recommend to her next nanny."

He was only responding to her teasing, but his words were a reminder to both of them that the summer was almost halfway over. And when it was done, Hannah would go back to her own life, and he and his daughter would go on with theirs.

Not so very long ago he'd been thinking about the two months he'd planned to spend at Cielo del Norte as an interminable amount of time. Now that the first month had nearly passed, it didn't seem long enough.

Hannah returned to the media room and resumed her

place at one end of the oversize leather sofa. He'd been sitting at the other end earlier, with Riley as a buffer between them, but he sat in the middle now.

She looked at him warily. "Don't you have phone calls to make or projects to complete?"

"It's almost ten o'clock."

"That hasn't seemed to matter on any other night."

She was right. He was in the habit of disappearing back into his office again as soon as he'd said good-night to his daughter. But what Hannah didn't know was that he often just sat behind his desk, doing nothing much of anything except ensuring that he kept a safe and careful distance between himself and the far-too-tempting nanny. And if he was smart, he would have done the same thing tonight, except that he'd made his daughter a promise.

"Riley asked me to keep an eye on you."

"I'm fine," she insisted.

"She made me pinky-swear," he told her.

Her lips curved. "It's sweet of her to worry, but I'm not concussed and I don't need anyone watching over me."

"I know it," he acknowledged. "But Riley seems really concerned."

"A lot of kids are preoccupied by death and dying," she said. "I would guess it's even more usual for a child who's lost someone close."

Somehow he knew that she wasn't just talking about Riley anymore. "How old were you when your mom died?" he asked.

"Eight."

"What happened?"

"There was a malaria epidemic in the village where we were living at the time. I got sick first, and my mom didn't trust that the Swazi doctors knew what they were doing, so she called Phillip. By the time he arrived, I was on my way to recovery, but—" Her gaze shifted away, but not before he caught a glimpse of the moisture in her eyes. "But while she'd been taking care of me, she'd ignored her own symptoms. By the time the doctors realized that she'd been infected, too, the disease had progressed too far."

She tucked her feet up beneath her on the sofa. "I thought my dad blamed me," she confided. "And that's why he sent me away after she died."

"He sent you away?"

"No one admitted that's what happened. Uncle Phillip said that I would be better off in Tesoro del Mar, that traveling from village to village was no kind of life for a child, and my father agreed. But no one had seemed too concerned about that while my mom was alive, and no one seemed to think about the fact that they were sending me away to live with a man I barely even knew."

"I'm sorry, Hannah."

And he was. He couldn't imagine how traumatic it had been for a child who'd just lost her mother to be taken away from her only other parent.

"I'm not. At the time, I was devastated," she admitted. "But now I realize it was the best thing that could have happened. My uncle gave me not just a home, but a sense of stability and security I'd never had before. He was—and is—a constant presence in my life, the one person I know I can depend on above all others."

"Where's your father now?"

"Botswana, I think. At least, that's where his last email came from."

"The one that told you he was getting married again," he guessed.

"How did you know about that?"

"You once told me that you wanted me to work on my relationship with Riley so that she didn't get an email from me telling her that she had a new stepmother."

She winced. "I was upset. The message wasn't that he

was getting married but that he'd already gotten married. He didn't even think to tell me beforehand. And probably the only reason he thought to share the news at all is that they're coming to Tesoro del Mar in the fall and he hopes I'll get a chance to meet her."

"I can see how that would have pulled the proverbial rug out from under you," he admitted.

"But it shouldn't have," she said now. "Because the truth is, I don't know him well enough to be surprised by anything he does. In the past eighteen years, since Uncle Phillip brought me here, I've only seen my father half a dozen times.

"His work has always been more important to him than anything else. And I guess, when you trust that you've been called to a higher mission, it needs to be a priority," she acknowledged. "And I know he believes in what he's doing. He goes to the darkest corners of the world, he sees families living in poverty and he sees children struggling to learn, but he never saw me."

She sighed. "It hurt. For a long time. But I finally realized that he was doing what he needed to do, because the people he helps out need him more than I ever did."

He didn't think it was as simple as that, and he was furious with her father for turning a blind eye to the needs of his child and angry with himself because he'd been doing the same thing to Riley. And he was so very grateful to Hannah for making him see it and helping him to be a better father to his daughter.

"So will you go to meet her—your father's new wife?"

"Probably." Her lips curved just a little.

He lifted a brow, silently inquiring.

"My friend Karen suggested I show up with a husband in tow," she explained.

"Getting married just to make a point seems a little extreme, don't you think?"

"More than a little, but I don't think she was suggesting an actual legal union."

"Have you ever been married?" he asked curiously.

"No."

"Engaged?"

"Haven't we covered enough of my family history for one night?"

He figured that was a *yes,* but decided to respect her wish not to talk about it. At least for now. "So what are we going to talk about for the rest of the night?"

"If you're really determined to hang out here babysitting me, that's your choice, Your Highness. But I'm going to watch some television."

"It's my choice," he agreed. "And it's my TV." And he snapped up the remote before she could.

She narrowed her gaze. "Don't make me wrestle you for it."

"Would you really?" He was certainly willing to let her tackle him. In fact, the more he thought about it, the more intrigued he was by the possibility.

"I would, but I'm supposed to be resting."

Another fantasy ruined, he handed her the remote.

Chapter Twelve

The rain was pouring down when Michael pulled into the drive at Cielo del Norte after a quick trip into town to meet with an old friend. It had been gray and drizzling for the better part of three days, but now the skies had completely opened up.

As he ran through the deluge to the front door, a flash of lightning split the sky, almost immediately followed by a crash of thunder. He winced, knowing how much Riley hated storms. If she was awakened by one in the night, he'd sometimes find her trying to crawl under the covers of his bed, her eyes squeezed tight and her hands pressed against her ears.

Inside, he shook the rain off of his coat and hung it in the closet. From the kitchen, he could smell the mouthwatering scents of roasted pork and sweet potatoes, but it was the music he heard in the distance that drew him down the hall.

Not surprisingly, it was coming from the music room. But

it certainly wasn't Riley practicing piano. In fact, it wasn't anything he had ever heard before. And when he pushed open the door, he saw something that he was certain he'd never seen before.

Riley was dancing—spinning and twirling, with her arms flying and her legs kicking. Hannah was right into the music with her, hips wriggling and body shimmying. And both of them were singing at the tops of their lungs about…he wasn't sure if he was unable to decipher the lyrics or if they just didn't make any sense, but both his daughter and her nanny seemed to know all the words.

He winced at the volume of the music, but he knew there was no way that Riley could hear the thunder over whatever it was that they were listening to—and no way they could have heard him enter the room. So he just leaned back against the wall and enjoyed the show for a few minutes.

One song led into the next, and they continued to sing and laugh and dance, and he continued to watch, marveling at the sheer happiness that radiated from his little girl. He couldn't remember ever seeing her like this—just being silly and having fun, and he realized that Hannah had been right about this, too. His daughter, despite all of her talents and gifts, needed a chance to simply be a child.

Impossible as it seemed, Riley's smile grew even wider when she finally spotted him.

"Look, Daddy! We're dancing!"

While Riley continued to move, Hannah's steps faltered when she realized that she and the child were no longer alone, and he would have bet that the flush in her cheeks was equal parts embarrassment and exertion.

"Don't let me interrupt," he said. "Please."

But she went to the boom box and lowered the volume, at least a little.

He picked up the CD case, looked at the cover, then lifted his brows.

"Grace let Riley borrow it," she told him, then grinned. "In exchange, Riley gave her a copy of Stravinsky's *Rite of Spring*."

He was suprised to learn that his little girl, who had a profound appreciation for the classics, could find such pleasure in jumping up and down and wiggling her hips to something called *Yo Gabba Gabba*, but he wasn't at all disappointed by the recent changes in her behavior.

"So what precipitated this dance-a-thon?"

"The precipitation," Hannah said, and smiled. "The rain made us give up on the idea of going outside, but Riley had a lot of energy to burn off."

"She's changed so much in only a few weeks," he noted.

"You say that in a way that I'm not sure if you approve or disapprove of the changes," she said uncertainly.

"I approve," he assured her. "I guess I'm still just getting used to it. I would never have said that she was unhappy before—but I've also never seen her as obviously happy as she is now. And to hear her laugh—the sound is so pure and full of joy."

"She's a wonderful little girl," Hannah assured him.

He had to smile, remembering that it hadn't been so long ago that she'd warned him that his daughter was turning into a spoiled brat. But then she'd taken Riley out of the familiar, structured world that she knew and changed all of the rules.

And while there had been a few growing pains in the beginning—and he was sure there would be more to come—he couldn't deny that he was impressed by the results.

"With a real passion for dance," the nanny continued.

Watching his daughter move, he couldn't deny that it was true. She might not have a natural talent, but she certainly had enthusiasm.

"My sister has a friend who—"

"No," Hannah interrupted quickly, then softened her refusal with a smile.

He frowned. "How do you even know what I was going to say?"

"Because I know how your mind works. And Riley doesn't need any more lessons. At least, not yet. Just let her have some fun for a while. And then, if she does want more formal training, enroll her in a class where she can learn along with other kids."

When the current song came to an end, Hannah snapped the music off.

"It's not done," Riley protested. "There's still three more songs."

"How many times has she listened to this CD?" Michael wondered.

"I've lost count," Hannah admitted. Then to Riley she said, "It's almost time for dinner, so you need to go wash up."

The little girl collapsed into a heap on the floor. "I'm too tired."

Michael had to smile. "If you're not too tired to keep dancing, you can't be too tired to twist the taps on a faucet," he said, picking her up off of the floor to set her on her feet. "Go on."

With a weary sigh, the princess headed off.

Hannah took the CD out of the machine and returned it to its case.

"Did you have any formal dance training?" he asked curiously.

She nodded, a smile tugging at the corners of her mouth. "Ballet, because my uncle Phillip was a lot like you in that he wanted to give me every possible opportunity. But after two years, my teacher told him that she couldn't in good conscience continue to take his money when it was obvious that I had less than zero talent."

"She did not say that," Michael protested.

"She did," Hannah insisted. "And truthfully, I was relieved."

"You looked pretty good to me when you were spinning around with Riley."

"We were just having fun."

"Will you dance with me?" he asked her.

She looked up, surprise and wariness in her eyes. "Wh-what?"

He moved to the CD player, pressed the button for the satellite radio—and jumped back when heavy metal screamed out at him. Hannah laughed while he adjusted the volume and scrolled through the preset channels until he found a familiar song.

"This one was at the top of the charts in my first year of college," he told her, and offered his hand.

"I don't recognize it," she admitted.

"Then I won't have to worry about you trying to lead," he teased.

Though she still looked hesitant, she finally put her hand in his.

"You really don't know this song?" he asked, after they'd been dancing for about half a minute.

She shook her head.

"Okay, now I have to ask—how old are you, Hannah?"

"Twenty-six."

Which meant that she was a dozen years younger than he, and while he'd been in college, she'd still been in grade school. But that was a long time ago, and there was no doubt that she was now all grown up. And soft and feminine and undeniably sexy.

He drew in a breath and the scent of her invaded his senses and clouded his mind.

"Hannah—"

She tipped her head back to meet his gaze, and whatever

words he'd intended to say flew out of his mind when he looked into those blue-gray eyes and saw the desire he felt reflected back at him.

He'd been fighting his feelings for her from the beginning, and to what effect? He still wanted her, now more than ever. And if she wanted him, too—and the look in her eyes made him believe that she did—then what was the harm in letting the attraction between them follow through to its natural conclusion?

They were, after all, both adults...but the little girl peeking around the corner was definitely not.

"Caridad said to tell you that it's dinnertime," Riley announced.

Hannah wanted to scream with frustration.

For just a minute, she'd been sure that the prince was going to kiss her again. And his gaze, when it flickered back to her now, was filled with sincere regret.

Regret that they'd been interrupted?

Or regret that he'd almost repeated the "mistake" of a few weeks earlier?

"Thank you for the dance, Hannah," he said formally.

"It was my pleasure, Your Highness."

He lifted her hand to kiss it.

She wanted a real kiss—not some lame fairy-tale facsimile. But then his lips brushed the back of her hand, and she felt the tingles all the way down to her toes.

It wasn't the passionate lip-lock with full frontal contact that she craved, but it wasn't exactly lame, either. And that made her wonder: if a casual touch could wield such an impact, what would happen if the man ever really touched her?

She was almost afraid to find out—and more afraid that she never would.

* * *

The next day, the sun shone clear and bright in the sky. After being cooped up for the better part of three days, Riley was thrilled to get outside and run around. In the morning, Hannah took her for a long walk on the beach. Michael watched from his office as they fed the gulls and wrote messages in the sand, and he wished he was with them.

He tore his attention from the window and back to his work. He was putting the final touches on a project for the upcoming National Diabetes Awareness Campaign, and if he finished it up this morning, then he could spend the whole afternoon with Riley and Hannah.

He wasn't sure when he'd started thinking of Hannah as Hannah and not "Miss Castillo" or his daughter's nanny— or when he'd started looking forward to spending time with her, too. In the beginning, when every step in his relationship with Riley seemed both awkward and tentative, he'd been grateful for her guidance. But somewhere along the line, he'd begun to enjoy her company and thought they might actually be friends. Except that he was still fighting against his body's desire to get her naked.

He pushed that idea from his mind and forced himself to get back to work.

He did finish the project by lunch, and afterward Riley invited him down to the beach to build castles in the sand. It was an offer he couldn't refuse, and he wasn't just surprised but disappointed when Hannah begged off. She claimed to want to catch up on some emails, but he knew that she was really trying to give him some one-on-one time with his daughter.

He appreciated her efforts. After all, she was only going to be with them until the end of the summer, at which time he and Riley were going to have to muddle through on their own—or muddle through the adjustment period with another new nanny. The thought made him uneasy, but he refused to delve too deeply into the reasons why. It was easier to believe that he was concerned about his daughter than to acknowledge that he might actually miss Hannah when she was gone.

After castle-building, they went swimming to wash the sand off, then Riley talked him into whacking some balls around the court with her. Hannah had told him that Riley was learning a lot from Kevin, and he was pleased to see that it was true. By the time they were finished on the court, he noticed that Hannah had come outside and was sitting on one of the lounge chairs on the terrace.

Riley spotted her at almost the same moment, and she went racing ahead. By the time Michael had reached the bottom step, his daughter was already at the top. Then she climbed right up into her nanny's lap and rested her head against her shoulder.

"It looks like you wore her out on the tennis court," Hannah said to him.

"She's had a busy day," he noted, dropping down onto the edge of the other chair.

Riley nodded her head, her eyes already starting to drift shut. "I'm ready for quiet time now."

Hannah smiled at his daughter's code word for "nap." "Quiet time's okay," she agreed. "But you can't fall asleep because it's going to be time for dinner soon."

The little girl yawned. "I'm not hungry."

"Caridad was making lasagna," Michael reminded her. "And that's one of your favorites."

"Is Hannah going to burn the garlic bread again?"

The nanny sighed. "I'm never going to live that down, am I?"

His daughter giggled.

"Well, in answer to your question, I can promise you that I am *not* going to burn the garlic bread because Caridad won't let me in the kitchen while she's cooking anymore."

"I'm glad," Riley said. "Because if you were helping her cook, you couldn't be here with me."

Hannah's lips curved as the little girl snuggled against her, but the smile faltered as she caught Michael's gaze.

"Is something wrong?" she asked quietly.

"What?" He realized he was scowling, shook his head. "No."

But he could tell that she was unconvinced, and he couldn't blame her. Because the truth was, *everything* about this situation was wrong.

She shouldn't be there. She shouldn't be on *that* chair on *this* deck cuddling with his daughter. That was *Sam's* chair—he'd painted it that particularly garish shade of lime green because Sam had thought it was a fun color. And this was *their* special place—where they used to come to escape the craziness of the world together. And Riley was *their* little girl—the child that his wife had given her life to bring into the world.

He felt a pang in his chest. Caridad was right—Riley needed more than a nanny, she needed her mother. But that was something he couldn't give her. Sam was gone. Forever.

He thought he'd accepted that fact. After almost four years, he should have accepted it. During that entire time, while he'd gone through the motions of living, he'd been confident that Riley was in good hands with Brigitte, and he'd been comfortable with his daughter's relationship with her nanny.

So why did it seem so different when that nanny was someone else? Why did seeing his daughter with Hannah seem so wrong? Or was the problem maybe that it seemed so right?

How was it possible that after only one month, Hannah had become such an integral part of his daughter's life—and his, too? It was hard to believe that it had been four weeks already, that it was already the beginning of August, almost…

The third of August.

The pain was like a dagger through his heart. The stab of accompanying guilt equally swift and strong. He reached for the railing, his fingers gripping so tight that his knuckles were white.

Dios—he'd almost forgotten.

How had he let that happen? How had the events of the past few weeks so thoroughly occupied his mind and his heart that the date had very nearly escaped him?

He drew in a deep breath, exhaled it slowly.

"I just remembered that there are some files I need from the office," he announced abruptly. "I'll have to go back to Port Augustine."

"Tonight?" Hannah asked incredulously.

"Can we go, too, Daddy?" Riley asked.

Not *I* but *we,* he realized, and felt another pang. Already she was so attached to Hannah, maybe too attached. Because at the end of the summer, Riley would have to say goodbye to someone else she cared about.

"Not this time," he told her, stroking a finger over the soft curve of her cheek. "It would be too far past your bedtime before we got into town."

"When are you coming back?" Riley asked.

"Tomorrow," he promised.

Riley nodded, her head still pillowed on Hannah's shoulder. "Okay."

"Are you sure everything's all right?" Hannah asked.

Concern was evident in her blue-gray gaze, and as Michael looked into her eyes, he suddenly couldn't even remember what color Sam's had been.

"I'm sure," he lied.

He'd loved his wife—he *still* loved his wife—but the memories were starting to fade. She'd been the center of his world for so many years, and it had taken him a long time to put his life back together after she was gone. Losing her had absolutely devastated him, and that was something he wouldn't ever let himself forget. And that was why he wouldn't ever risk loving someone else.

Chapter Thirteen

Michael didn't remember many of the details of Sam's funeral. He didn't even remember picking out the plot where she was buried, and he wasn't entirely sure that he had. It was probably Marissa, who had stepped in to take care of all of the details—and his baby girl—who made the decision.

Thinking back to that time now, he knew that Sam would have been disappointed in him. She would have expected him to be there for their daughter, and he hadn't been. Not for a long time.

But he was trying to be there for her now, trying to be the father his little girl needed, and he thought he'd been making some progress. There was no awkwardness with Riley anymore. Not that everything was always smooth sailing, but they were learning to navigate the stormy seas together.

Hannah was a big part of that, of course. There was no denying the role she'd played in bringing him and Riley together. And sitting here now, on the little wrought-iron bench by his wife's grave as he'd done so many times before, he knew that Sam would be okay with that.

He caught a flicker of movement in the corner of his eye and, glancing up, saw his sister climbing the hill. She laid the bouquet of flowers she carried in front of Sam's stone.

"Are you doing okay?" she asked gently.

"You know, I really think I am."

She nodded at that, then took a seat beside him.

They sat in silence for a few more minutes, before he asked, "Why did you come?"

"Did you want to be alone?"

"No, I just wondered why you were here. Why you always seem to be there when I need you—and even when I don't realize that I do."

"Because you're my big brother and I love you."

He slipped his arm across her shoulders. "I'm the luckiest brother in the world."

She tipped her head back and smiled.

"It would have been our sixteenth anniversary today," he said.

"I know."

"I thought we would have sixty years together." He swallowed around the lump in his throat. "She was more than my wife, she was my best friend—and the best part of my life. And then she was gone."

"But now you have Riley," his sister reminded him.

He nodded. "The best part of both of us."

Marissa smiled again. "I heard she's learning to play tennis."

"Dr. Marotta told you, I'll bet."

She nodded. "How's Hannah?"

"The stitches should come out in a couple of days, and she's learned to keep a distance from Riley's backhand." He waited a beat, then said, "She canceled almost all of Riley's lessons for the summer."

"Good for her."

He hadn't expected such unequivocal support of the decision. "You were the one who encouraged me to find a piano instructor for Riley," he reminded her.

"Because she has an obvious talent that should be nurtured. But you went from music lessons twice a week to five days a week, then added language instruction and art classes. And I know the deportment classes were Mother's idea, but you could have said no. Instead, the poor child barely had time to catch her breath."

Which was almost exactly what Hannah had said. And while Riley never complained about her schedule, he should have seen that it was too much. He should have seen a lot of things he'd been oblivious to until recently.

"So other than tennis, what is Riley doing with her spare time?" his sister wanted to know.

"She's...having fun."

"You sound surprised."

"I'd almost forgotten what it sounded like to hear her laugh," he admitted. "It's...magic."

Marissa smiled again. "Maybe I was wrong."

"About what?"

"To worry about you. Maybe you are beginning to heal."

He knew that he was. And yet, he had to admit, "I still miss her."

"Of course," she agreed. "But you've got to move on. You're too young to be alone for the rest of your life."

"I can't imagine being with anyone other than Sam," Michael told her, but even as he spoke the words, he knew that they weren't entirely true. The truth was, he'd never loved anyone but Sam, and it seemed disloyal to even think that he ever could.

But that didn't stop him from wanting Hannah.

* * *

Hannah had sensed that something was wrong when the prince suddenly insisted that he needed to go to Port Augustine the night before. It seemed apparent to her that what he really needed was to get away from Cielo del Norte, though she couldn't figure out why.

Over the past few weeks, as Michael and Riley had spent more time together and grown closer, she'd thought that she and the prince were growing closer, too. But his abrupt withdrawal suggested otherwise.

She wasn't surprised that he was gone overnight. It didn't make sense to make the drive back when he had a house in town. She was surprised when he stayed away through all of the next day. But Caridad seemed unconcerned about his whereabouts. In fact, the housekeeper didn't comment on his absence at all, leading Hannah to suspect that she might know where the prince was.

It was only Riley, because she'd been spending more and more time with him every day, who asked for her daddy. Hannah tried to reassure the child without admitting that she had no idea where the prince had gone—or when he would be back.

It was late—hours after Riley had finally settled down to sleep—before she heard the door open. She told herself that she wasn't waiting up for him, but she'd taken the draft of Kevin's latest essay into the library to read because she knew if she was there that she would hear the prince come in.

"I didn't know if you'd still be up," he said.

"I had some things to do."

He opened a glass cabinet and pulled out a crystal decanter of brandy. She wasn't in the habit of drinking anything stronger than wine, and never more than a single glass. But when the prince poured a generous splash of the dark amber liquid into each of two snifters and offered one to her, it seemed rude to refuse.

"You haven't asked where I've been all day," he noted, swirling the brandy in his glass.

"I figured if you wanted me to know, you'd tell me."

He sat down on the opposite end of the sofa, but with his back to the arm, so that he was facing her. But he continued to stare into his glass as he said, "It was Sam's and my anniversary today."

"You went to the cemetery," she guessed.

"Just like I do every year." He swallowed a mouthful of brandy before he continued. "Except that this is the first time I almost forgot."

Hannah eyed him warily, uncertain how to respond—or even if she should. She sipped her drink cautiously while she waited for him to continue.

"We celebrated twelve anniversaries together. This is only the fourth year that she's been gone, and the date almost slipped by me."

"You're feeling guilty," she guessed.

"Maybe," he acknowledged. He tipped the glass to his lips again. "And maybe I'm feeling relieved, too. Because in the first year that she was gone, I couldn't seem to not think, every single day, about how empty my life was without her, so the important dates—like her birthday and our anniversary—were unbearable."

He looked into his glass, and frowned when he found that it was nearly empty. "And then there was Mother's Day. She wanted nothing so much as she wanted to have a baby, and she never got to celebrate a single Mother's Day."

Beneath the bitter tone, she knew that he was still hurting deeply, still grieving for the wife he'd loved.

"I wasn't happy when Sam told me she was pregnant," he admitted.

Coming from a man who obviously doted on his little

girl, the revelation startled her more than anything else he'd said.

"I knew it was a risk for her," he explained, and rose to pour another splash of brandy into his glass. "Though she'd successfully managed her diabetes for years, the doctors warned that pregnancy and childbirth would take a toll on her body.

"After a lot of discussion and numerous medical consults, we decided not to take the risk. It was enough, I thought, that we had each other."

Obviously, Hannah realized, at some point that decision had changed.

"She didn't tell me that she'd stopped taking her birth control pills," Michael confided. "We'd always been partners—not just in the business but in our marriage. Neither one of us made any major decisions without consulting the other, so I wasn't just surprised when she told me that we were going to have a baby, I was furious."

Hannah didn't say anything, because she knew the prince wasn't trying to make conversation so much as he was trying to vent the emotions that were tearing him up inside. So she just sat and listened and quietly sipped her drink.

"I was furious with Sam," he continued, "for unilaterally making the decision that would cost her life, even if neither of us knew that at the time. And I was furious with my mother, for convincing Sam that I needed an heir—because I found out later that was the motivation behind Sam's deception."

And that, she thought, explained so much of the tension in his relationship with his mother.

"But in the end, I realized that I was most furious with myself—because I should have taken steps to ensure that Sam couldn't get pregnant. If I had done that, then I wouldn't have lost my wife."

He sank into the chair beside hers, as if all of the energy

and emotion had drained out of him so that he was no longer able to stand.

She touched his hand. "You might not have lost your wife," she agreed softly. "But then you wouldn't have your little girl."

He sighed. "You're right. And now, when I think about it, I know that even if I could go back in time, I wouldn't want to. I couldn't ever give up Riley, even if it meant I could have Sam back."

"They say there's nothing as strong as a parent's love for a child," she said softly, her throat tight.

"The first time I held her in my arms, I knew there wasn't anything I wouldn't do for her," he admitted. "For a few glorious hours, I let myself imagine the future we would have together—Sam and Riley and myself. And then Sam was gone."

The grief in his voice was still raw—even after almost four years. And listening to him talk about the wife he'd obviously loved with his whole heart, Hannah experienced a pang of envy. Would she ever know how it felt to love like that—and to be loved like that in return?

She'd thought she was in love with Harrison, but when their relationship ended, she was more angry than hurt. She most definitely had *not* been heartbroken.

"I'm sorry," he said. "I didn't come in here with the intention of dumping on you."

"Please don't apologize, Your Highness. And don't worry—I can handle a little dumping."

"Strong shoulders and a soft heart?"

She managed a smile. "Something like that."

"Can you handle one more confession?"

She would sit here with him forever if it was what he wanted, but she had no intention of admitting that to him, so she only said, "Sure."

"I met Sam when I was fifteen years old and while I

didn't realize it at the time, I started to fall for her that very same day. I was lucky enough that she fell in love with me, too, because from that first moment, there was never anyone else. Even after she died...I never wanted anyone else." His dark eyes lifted to hers, held. "Until now."

She swallowed.

"I know it's wrong," he continued. "Not that it's a betrayal of my vows, because I've finally accepted that Sam is gone, but wrong because you're Riley's nanny and—"

She lifted a hand to touch her fingers to his lips, cutting off his explanation. She didn't want to hear him say why it was wrong—she refused to believe that it was. If he wanted her even half as much as she wanted him, that was all that mattered.

Somewhere in the back of her mind it occurred to her that the prince was still grieving and that if she made the next move, she might be taking advantage of him in a vulnerable moment.

Then his fingers encircled her wrist, and his thumb stroked slowly over the pulse point there as if to gauge her response. As if he couldn't hear how hard and fast her heart was pounding. Then he lowered her hand and laid it against his chest, so that she could feel that his heart was pounding just as hard and fast, and the last of her reservations dissipated.

She knew there was no future for them, but if she could have even one night, she would gladly take it and cherish the memories forever.

"I want you, Hannah," he said again. "But the first time I kissed you, I promised that I wouldn't do it again."

"You promised that you wouldn't make any unwanted advances," she corrected softly.

"Isn't that the same thing?"

"Not if I want you to kiss me," she said.

"Do you?" he asked, his mouth hovering above hers so

that she only needed to tilt her chin a fraction to make the kiss happen.

"Yes." She whispered her response against his mouth.

It was the barest brush of her lips against his, yet she felt the jolt all the way down to her toes. She caught only a hint of his flavor, but she knew that it was rich and dark and more potent than the brandy she'd sipped.

"I want you to kiss me," she repeated, in case there was any doubt.

He responded by skimming his tongue over the bow of her upper lip, making her sigh with pleasure. With need.

"I want you," she said.

His tongue delved beneath her parted lips, tasting, teasing. She met him halfway, in a slow dance of seduction.

It was only their second kiss, and yet she felt as if she'd kissed him a thousand times before. She felt as if she belonged in his arms. With him. Forever.

No—she wasn't going to let herself pretend that this was some kind of fairy tale. She knew better than to think that the prince wanted to sweep her off of her feet and take her away to live out some elusive happily-ever-after.

But he did sweep her off of her feet—to carry her up the stairs to her bedroom. And the sheer romanticism of the gesture made her heart sigh.

"Say my name, Hannah."

It seemed an odd request, until she realized that she'd never spoken his name aloud. Maybe because she hoped that using his title would help her keep him at a distance. But she didn't want any distance between them now.

"Michael," she whispered, savoring the sound of his name on her lips.

He smiled as he laid her gently on the bed, then made quick work of the buttons that ran down the front of her blouse. She shivered when he parted the material, exposing her heated flesh to the cool air. And again when he pushed the silk off of her shoulders and dipped his head to skim his lips over the ridge of her collarbone.

"Are you cold?"

She shook her head.

How could she be cold when there was so much heat pulsing through her veins? When her desire for him was a burning need deep in the pit of her belly?

His mouth moved lower. He released the clasp at the front of her bra and pushed the lacy cups aside, exposing her breasts to the ministrations of his lips and teeth and tongue.

She wasn't a virgin, but no one had ever touched her the way he was touching her. The stroke of his hands was somehow both lazy and purposeful, as if he wanted nothing more than to show her how much he wanted her. And with every brush of his lips and every touch of his fingertips, she felt both desire and desired.

Her hands raced over him, eagerly, desperately. She tore at his clothes, tossed them aside. She wanted to explore his hard muscles, to savor the warmth of his skin, to know the intimacy of his body joined with hers.

Obviously he wanted the same thing, because he pulled away from her only long enough to strip away the last of his clothes and take a small square packet from his pocket.

"I didn't plan for this to happen tonight," he told her. "But lately…well, I began to hope it would happen eventually and I wanted to be prepared."

"I'm glad one of us was," she assured him.

His fingers weren't quite steady as he attempted to open the package, and he dropped it twice. The second time, he swore so fervently she couldn't hold back a giggle. But he finally managed to sheath himself and rejoined her on the bed, nudging her thighs apart so that he could lower himself between them.

"Will you do me a favor?" he asked.

"What's that?"

"When you remember this night, will you edit out that part?"

She smiled. "Absolutely."

But it was a lie. She had no intention of editing out any of the parts. She wanted to remember every little detail of every minute that she had with Michael. Because she didn't have any illusions. She knew this couldn't last. Maybe not even beyond this one night. But she wasn't going to think about that now. She wasn't going to ask for more than he could give. She was just going to enjoy the moment and know that it was enough.

His tongue swirled around her nipple, then he drew the aching peak into his mouth and suckled, and she gasped with shock and pleasure. He shifted his attention to her other breast, making her gasp again.

Oh yes, this was enough.

Then his mouth found hers again in a kiss that tasted of hunger and passion. His tongue slid deep into her mouth, then slowly withdrew. Advance and retreat. It was a sensual tease designed to drive her wild, and it was succeeding.

She whimpered as she instinctively shifted her hips, aching for the hard length of him between her thighs. Deep inside her.

She rocked against him, wordlessly pleading.

He entered her in one hard thrust, and her release was just as hard and fast. Wave after wave of pleasure crashed over her with an unexpected intensity that left her baffled and breathless.

While her body was riding out the last aftershocks of pleasure, he began to move inside of her. Slow, steady strokes that started the anticipation building all over again.

Had she honestly thought that this might not be enough?

It was so much more than she'd expected, more than she'd even dared hope for, more than enough. And still, he somehow managed to give her more, to demand more, until it wasn't just enough—it was too much.

His thrusts were harder and faster now, and so deep she felt as if he was reaching into the very center of her soul. Harder and faster and deeper, until everything seemed to shatter in an explosion of heat and light and unfathomable pleasure.

Michael didn't know if he could move. He did know that he didn't want to. His heart was still pounding like a jackhammer and every muscle in his body ached, and yet he couldn't remember ever feeling so good. So perfectly content to be right where he was.

But his own contentment aside, he knew that Hannah probably couldn't breathe with his weight sprawled on top of her. So he summoned enough energy to roll off of her. But he kept one arm draped across her waist, holding her close to his side. After another minute, he managed to prop himself up on an elbow so that he could look at her.

Her hair was spread out over the pillow, her eyes were closed, her lips were slightly curved. She looked as if she'd been well and truly ravished, and he felt a surge of pure satisfaction that he'd had the pleasure of ravishing her. And he wanted to do so again.

He stroked a finger down her cheek. Her eyelids slowly lifted, her lips parted on a sigh.

"*Dios,* you're beautiful."

She smiled at that. "Postcoital rose-colored glasses."

He shook his head. "Maybe I've never told you that before, but it's true. Your skin is so soft and smooth, your lips are like pink rose petals and your eyes are all the shades of the stormy summer sky."

"I didn't realize you had such a romantic streak, Your Highness," she teased.

"Neither did I." His hand skimmed up her torso, from her

waist to her breast, his thumb stroking over the tight bud
of her nipple. "I always thought everything was black or
white—and for the past few years, there's been a lot more
black than white. And then you came along and gave me a
whole new perspective on a lot of things."

She arched into his palm, as if she wanted his touch as
much as he wanted to touch her. She had incredible breasts.
They were so full and round, and so delightfully responsive
to his touch.

Sam's curves had been much more modest, and she'd
often lamented her tomboy figure. Even when she'd been
pregnant, her breasts had never—

He froze.

Her gaze lifted to his, confusion swirling in the depths
of her blue-gray eyes.

"Michael?"

The unmistakable smoky tone of Hannah's voice snapped
him back to the present and helped him push aside any lin-
gering thoughts of Sam. As much as he'd loved his wife and
still grieved for the tragedy of a life cut so short, she was
his past and Hannah—

He wasn't entirely sure yet what Hannah would be to him,
but he knew that even if she wasn't his future, she was at
least his present.

He lowered his head to kiss her, softly, sweetly. And felt
the tension slowly seep out of her body.

Yes, she was definitely his present—an incredible gift.
The only woman he wanted right now. And so he used his
hands and his lips and his body and all of the hours until
the sun began to rise to convince her.

Chapter Fourteen

Hannah didn't expect that Michael would still be there when she woke up in the morning. She'd known he wouldn't stay through the night. There was no way he would risk his daughter finding him there. But it would have been nice to wake up in his arms. To make love with him again as the sun was streaming through the windows.

Making love with Michael had been the most incredible experience. He'd been attentive and eager and very thorough. She stretched her arms above her head, and felt her muscles protest. Very very thorough. But while her body was feeling all smug and sated, her mind was spinning.

She'd been fighting against her feelings for the prince since the beginning, and she knew that making love with him was hardly going to help her win that battle. But as she showered and got ready for the day, she knew she didn't regret it.

After breakfast, while Riley was in the music room practicing piano—simply because she wanted to—Hannah was in the kitchen sipping on her second cup of coffee while Caridad was making a grocery list.

"How many people are you planning to feed?" Hannah asked, when the housekeeper turned the page over to continue her list on the other side.

"Only the three of you," she admitted. "But I want to make several ready-to-heat meals that you can just take out of the freezer and pop in the microwave."

"Are you going somewhere?"

"Just for a few days, and I'm not sure when, but I want to be ready to go as soon as Loretta calls."

Loretta, Hannah remembered now, was Caridad and Estavan's second-oldest daughter who was expecting her first child—and their fourth grandchild. "When is she due?"

"The eighteenth of August."

"On Riley's birthday," Hannah noted.

"She mentioned that to you, did she?"

"Only about a thousand times," she admitted with a smile.

"A child's birthday is a big deal—or it should be." Caridad tapped her pen on the counter, her brow furrowed.

Hannah knew that there was more she wanted to say. She also knew that prompting and prodding wouldn't get any more information out of the housekeeper until she was ready. So she sipped her coffee while she waited.

"The princess is going to be four years old," Caridad finally said. "And she's never had a party."

Hannah was startled by this revelation, and then realized that she shouldn't be. Samantha had died within hours of giving birth, which meant that Riley's birthday was the same day that Michael had lost his wife.

"I don't mean to be critical—I know it's a difficult time for the prince. And it's not like her birthday passes without any kind of recognition.

"There's always a cake," Caridad continued. "Because I bake that myself. And presents. But she's never had a party."

"Why are you telling me?" Hannah asked warily.

"Because I think this year he might be ready, but he probably won't think of it on his own."

"You want me to drop some hints," she guessed.

The housekeeper nodded. "Yes, I think just a few hints would be enough."

"Okay, I'll try."

"But not too subtle," Caridad said. "Men sometimes don't understand subtle—they need to be hit over the head."

Hannah had to laugh. "I'll do my best."

Michael had thought that making love with Hannah once would be enough, but the first joining of their bodies had barely taken the edge off of his desire. After four years of celibacy, it probably wasn't surprising that his reawakened libido was in no hurry to hibernate again, but he knew that it wasn't as simple as that. He didn't just crave physical release, he craved Hannah.

Every time his path crossed with hers the following day, his hormones jolted to attention. Now that he knew what it was like to be with her—the sensual way she responded to the touch of his lips and his hands, the glorious sensation of sinking into her warm and welcoming body, the exquisite rhythm of their lovemaking—he wanted only to be with her again.

But what did *she* want?

He didn't have the slightest clue.

She'd been sleeping when he'd left her room, so he'd managed to avoid the awkward "What does this mean?" or "Where do we go from here?" conversations that purportedly followed first-time sex. Since Hannah was the first woman he'd been with since he'd started dating Sam almost eighteen years earlier, he had little firsthand experience with those morning-after moments. And now he didn't know what was the next step.

They had lunch and dinner together with Riley, as was customary, and the conversation flowed as easily as it usually did. There were no uncomfortable references to the previous night and no awkward silences. There was absolutely no indication at all that anything had changed between them.

Until later that night, when he left Riley's room after he was sure she was asleep, and he found Hannah in the hall.

It wasn't all that late, but she was obviously ready to turn in for the night. Her hair had been brushed so that it fell loose over her shoulders, and she was wearing a long blue silky robe that was cinched at her narrow waist. A hint of lace in the same color peeked through where the sides of the robe overlapped, piquing his curiosity about what she had on beneath the silky cover.

He'd intended to seek her out, to have the discussion they'd missed having the night before. But now that he'd found her, conversation was the last thing on his mind.

"Wow" was all he managed.

But apparently it was the right thing to say, because she smiled and reached for his hand. Silently, she drew him across the hall and into her room.

The robe was elegant but discreet, covering her from shoulders to ankles. But when he tugged on the belt and the silky garment fell open, he saw that what she wore beneath was a pure lace fantasy. A very little lace fantasy that barely covered her sexy curves, held into place by the skinniest of straps over her shoulders.

And while he took a moment to appreciate the contrast of her pale skin with the dark lace, he much preferred reality to fantasy. With one quick tug, he lifted the garment over her head and tossed it aside.

* * *

Afterward, he let her put the lace-and-silk fantasy back on, and they sat on her balcony with a bottle of wine, just watching the stars.

"Are you ever going to tell me about that engagement?" he asked her.

"It was a long time ago," she said dismissively.

Considering that she was only twenty-six, he didn't imagine that it could have been all that long ago, and he was too curious to drop the subject. "What happened?"

"It didn't work out."

He rolled his eyes.

"We met at university," she finally told him. "He was a member of the British aristocracy, I was not. As much as he claimed to love me, when his family made it clear that they disapproved of his relationship with a commoner, he ended it." There was no emotion in her voice, but he sensed that she wasn't as unaffected by the broken engagement as she tried to appear.

"How long were you together?"

"Almost four years." She lifted her glass to her lips. "They didn't seem concerned about my lack of pedigree so long as we were just dating—apparently even aristocrats are entitled to meaningless flings—but to marry me would have been a blight on the family tree."

Again, her recital was without emotion, but he saw the hurt in her eyes and silently cursed any man who could be so cruel and heartless to this incredible woman.

"I didn't imagine there was anyone living in the modern world—aside from my mother—" he acknowledged with a grimace "—who had such outdated views about maintaining the purity of bloodlines."

"And yet your mother married a farmer," Hannah mused.

"Elena is nothing if not illogical. Or maybe she believed that her royal genes would trump his." He smiled as an old memory nudged at his mind. "The first time I scraped my knee when I was a kid, I didn't know what the red stuff was, because I honestly believed that my blood was supposed to be blue."

She smiled, too, but there were clouds in her eyes, as if she was thinking of the lack of blue in her own veins.

"So did you at least get to keep the ring?" he asked, in an attempt to lighten the mood.

She shook her head. "It was a family heirloom," she explained dryly.

"He didn't actually ask for it back?"

"Before we even left the ancestral estate," she admitted.

"And you gave it to him?" He couldn't imagine that she would have just slid it off of her finger and handed it over. No, if she'd cared enough about the man to want to marry him, she wouldn't have been that cool about the end of their engagement.

"I threw it out the window."

He chuckled.

"It took him three hours on his hands and knees in the immaculately groomed gardens to find it."

"He must have been pissed."

"Harrison didn't have that depth of emotion," she informed him. "But he was 'most displeased' with my 'childish behavior.'"

"Sounds like you made a lucky escape." And he was glad, because if she'd married that pompous British twit, she wouldn't be here with him now.

"I know I did. I guess I just thought I'd be at a different place by this point in my life."

"You're only twenty-six," he reminded her. "And I don't think there are many places in the world better than this one."

"You know I didn't mean this place specifically." She

smiled as she tipped her head back to look up at the sky. "This place is…heaven."

"Cielo," he agreed. "And you are…*mi ángel*."

After almost a week had passed and Hannah's apparently too-subtle hints about Riley's approaching birthday continued to go unnoticed, she decided that Michael needed to be hit over the head. Not as literally as she had been, she thought, rubbing the pink scar that was the only visible reminder of her clash with Riley's racquet now that her stitches had been removed. But just as effectively.

So on Thursday morning, after the little girl had gone to the tennis court with Kevin, she cornered the prince in his office.

"It's Riley's birthday next week," she said.

"I know when her birthday is," he assured her.

"Well, I was thinking that it might be fun to have a party."

"A party?" he echoed, as if unfamiliar with the concept.

"You know—with a cake, party hats, noisemakers."

He continued to scribble notes on the ad layout on his desk. "Okay."

She blinked. "Really?"

He glanced up, a smile teasing the corners of his mouth. "Did you want me to say no?"

"Of course I didn't want you to say no," she told him. "But I thought there would be some discussion first."

He finally set down his pen and leaned back in his chair. "Discussion about what?"

"I don't know. Maybe the when and where, the guest list, a budget."

"When—sometime on the weekend. Where—here. As for the guest list, I figure if it's Riley's party, she should get to decide, and I don't care what it costs so long as I don't have to do anything but show up."

Happiness bubbled up inside of her. She couldn't wait to race into the kitchen and tell Caridad the good news.

"If you let Riley decide what she wants, it could turn into a very big party," she warned.

"I think we're overdue for a big party." He slipped his arms around her waist, drew her close. "And this year, I feel like celebrating."

Her heart bumped against her ribs, but she forced herself to respond lightly. "Okay, then. I'll talk to the birthday girl when she comes in and get started making plans."

"Where is Riley?"

"On the tennis court with Kevin."

"You'll have to give me an updated schedule," he said, not entirely teasing. "I never know where to find her these days."

"We don't have a schedule—we're improvising."

"I can improvise," he said, brushing his mouth against hers.

Hannah sighed. "Mmm. You're good at that."

"How long is she going to be busy with Kevin?"

"Probably about an hour. Why?"

"Because I want to show you some of the other things I'm good at."

Her cheeks flushed. "It's nine o'clock in the morning."

"But you don't have a schedule to worry about—you're improvising," he reminded her.

"Yes, but—"

"I really want to make love with you in the daylight."

He was a very lucky man, Michael thought with a grin as Hannah took his hand led him up to her room. And about to get luckier.

When he followed her through the door, his gaze automatically shifted toward the bed upon which they'd made love every night for the past nine days—and caught on the enormous bouquet of flowers in the vase on her bedside table.

He picked up the card. "With sincere thanks for helping me survive summer school, Kevin."

She paused in the process of removing the decorative throw cushions from the bed when she saw him holding the card. "Isn't that sweet?"

"Sure," he agreed stiffly. "He's finished his course, then?"

She nodded. "He got an A-plus on his final essay to finish with first-class honors."

"Caridad must be thrilled."

"She promised to make baklava, just for me," Hannah told him.

She said it as if that was her favorite, and maybe it was. He didn't know too much about what she liked or didn't like.

"I didn't know you liked flowers," he said, as if that was an excuse for the fact that he'd never thought to give her any.

"Who doesn't like flowers?" she countered lightly.

There was no accusation in her words, no judgment in her tone. Of course not—Hannah had made it clear from the beginning that she didn't have any expectations of him. Not even something as insignificant as a bouquet of flowers. And though he couldn't have said why, the realization annoyed him.

Or maybe he was annoyed to realize that he'd never really made an effort where Hannah was concerned. He'd never even taken her out to dinner, and they only went as far as the media room to watch a movie. They came together after dark like clandestine lovers, without ever having had anything that resembled a traditional date.

He knew that was his fault. He wasn't ready to subject Hannah to the media scrutiny of being seen in public together. Going shopping with Riley didn't really count, because the press accepted that the prince would require the assistance of a nanny when he was out with his daughter.

But he knew it would be very different if he and Hannah ventured out together without Riley as a buffer between them.

It was difficult to date when you were a member of the royal family, even one not in direct line to the throne. There was no such thing as privacy, and rarely even the pretense of it. Every appearance, every touch and kiss, became a matter of public speculation.

Not that Michael thought she couldn't handle it. He had yet to see Hannah balk at any kind of challenge. No, it was simply that he wasn't ready to go public with a relationship that felt too new, or maybe it was his feelings that were too uncertain. And that he was unwilling to look too deep inside himself to figure them out.

"I don't know if I like the idea of a much younger man bringing you flowers," he said, only half joking.

"He didn't just bring flowers," she teased. "He kissed me, too."

His brows drew together; Hannah laughed.

"It was a perfectly chaste peck on the cheek," she assured him.

"Lucky for him, or I might have to call him out for making a move on my woman."

Her brows rose. "*Your* woman?"

The words had probably surprised Michael even more than they'd surprised Hannah, and were followed by a quick spurt of panic. He immediately backtracked. "Well, you're mine until the end of summer, anyway."

Hannah turned away on the pretext of rearranging the colored bottles on her dresser, but not before he saw the light in her eyes fade. When she faced him again, her smile was overly bright.

"And that's less than three weeks away, so why are we wasting time talking?" She reached for the buttons on his shirt.

"Hannah—" He caught her hands, not sure what to say, or even if there were any words to explain how he felt about her.

He cared about her—he couldn't be with her if he didn't. And he didn't want her to think it was just sex, but he didn't want to give her false hope, either. He didn't want her to think that he could ever fall in love with her. Because he couldn't—he loved Sam.

"I never asked you for any promises," she told him.

And he couldn't have given them to her if she had. But he could give her pleasure, and he knew that doing so would give him pleasure, too.

He stripped her clothes away and lowered her onto the mattress. Then he knelt between her legs, stroking his fingertips slowly over the sensitive skin of her inner thighs. He brushed the soft curls at the apex of her thighs, and she gasped. He repeated the motion, parting the curls so that his thumb stroked over the nub at her center, and she bit down on her lip to keep from crying out.

"It's okay," he told her. "I want to hear you. I want to know how it feels when I touch you."

"It feels good. So good."

As his thumb circled her nub, he teased her slick, wet opening with the tip of a finger. She whimpered.

"Michael, please."

"Tell me what you want, Hannah."

"I want you."

He wanted her, too. He wanted to spread her legs wide and bury himself in her. To thrust into the hot wetness between her thighs, again and again, harder and faster, until he felt her convulse around him, dragging him into blissful oblivion.

But first, he wanted to taste her.

He slid his hands beneath her, lifting her hips off of the mattress so that he could take her with his mouth.

She gasped again, the sound reflecting both shock and pleasure. His tongue slid deep inside, reaching for the core of her feminine essence. Her breath was coming in quick, shallow pants, and he knew that she was getting close to her edge. It wouldn't have taken much to push her over the edge, but he wanted to draw out the pleasure for her—and for himself.

With his lips and his tongue, he probed and suckled and licked. He heard her breath quicken, then catch, and finally... release.

He stroked and kissed his way up her body until she was trembling again. Her belly, her breasts, her throat. She reached for him then, her fingers wrapping around and then sliding up the hard, throbbing length of him. He sucked in a breath. She stroked downward again, slowly, teasingly, until his eyes nearly crossed.

She arched her hips as she guided him to her center, welcoming him into her slick, wet heat. The last threads of his self-control slipped out of his grasp. He yanked her hips up and buried himself deep inside her.

She gasped and arched, pulling him even deeper, her muscles clamping around him as she climaxed again. The pulsing waves threatened to drag him under their wake. He reached for her hands, linking their fingers together over her head, making her his anchor as he rode out the tide of her release.

He waited until the pulses started to slow, then he began to move. She met him, stroke for stroke. Slow and deep. Then fast and hard. Faster. Harder. This time, when her release came, he let go and went with her.

Chapter Fifteen

Once the prince had given his nod of approval to the birthday party, Hannah was anxious to get started on the planning, so she turned to her best friend for advice. Karen outlined the five essential ingredients of a successful children's party: decorations, such as colorful streamers and balloons; games or crafts to keep the kids busy; cake to give the kids an unnecessary sugar high; presents for the guest of honor and loot bags for all of her friends—all of which should somehow coordinate with the party theme. And preferably, she added as an afterthought, outdoors so that the sugar-high kids weren't tearing through the house and destroying everything.

For Riley's first-ever birthday party, Hannah took her friend's list and gave it the royal treatment. She decided to go with a princess theme, since it was too obvious to resist.

The first glitch came when she asked Riley who she wanted to invite. The little girl mentioned her new friend, Grace, then added Kevin and Caridad and Estavan before rattling off the extensive list of all her aunts, uncles and cousins. She didn't mention her grandmother, and when Hannah asked about adding her to the list, the princess wrinkled her nose.

"Do I have to?"

"She is your grandmother, and you invited everyone else in the family," Hannah felt compelled to point out, even as she wondered if she was making a mistake.

But she couldn't help remembering Michael's comment about his mother barely knowing his daughter, and though she didn't think an invitation to one birthday party was likely to change that, she couldn't help hoping that it might be a start. And maybe, if the princess royal got to know Riley, she would give up on the idea of sending her away to boarding school.

"Everyone else in my family is nice," Riley said simply.

Hannah didn't quite know how to respond to that. She'd never actually met the princess royal and she didn't want to prejudge, but the princess's response made her wary.

"Would it be nice to invite everyone except her?" she prodded gently.

"No." Riley sighed, and considered her dilemma for another minute before she finally said, "Okay, you can put her on the list. But she doesn't get a loot bag."

After the guest list was finalized, Hannah turned her attention to other details. Taking her friend's advice to heart and unwilling to trust in the capriciousness of the weather, she rented a party tent to ensure that the celebration remained outside. Of course, when she called about the tent, she realized that she needed tables and chairs for inside the tent, and cloths to cover the tables and dress up the chairs. By the time she got off the phone, she was grateful the prince wasn't worried about budget.

"I just ordered a bouncy castle," she admitted to Caridad.

The housekeeper's brows lifted. "One of those big inflat-able things?"

"It fits the princess theme," she explained.

"Riley will love it."

"And a cotton-candy cart and popcorn machine."

Caridad's lips twitched. "Apparently you know how to throw a party."

"You don't think it's too much?"

"Of course it's too much, but after waiting four years for a party, it should be a party worth waiting for."

"It will be," Hannah said confidently.

And it was. The tent was decorated with thousands of tiny white fairy lights and hundreds of pink streamers and doz-ens of enormous bouquets of white and pink helium-filled balloons.

The younger female guests got to make their own tiaras—decorating foam crowns with glittery "jewels" and sparkling flowers. Thankfully Hannah had realized that the crowns wouldn't be a big hit with Riley's male cousins, so they got to decorate foam swords. After the craft, they played party games: pin the tail on the noble steed, musical thrones and a variation of Hot Potato with a glass slipper in place of the potato. And, of course, they spent hours just jumping around in the inflatable bouncy castle that had been set up behind the tennis court.

For a minute, Hannah had actually worried that Michael's mother was going to have a coronary when she spotted it. The princess royal had gone red in the face and demanded that the "grotesque monstrosity" be removed from the grounds immediately. But Michael had been unconcerned and simply ignored her demand, for which the kids were unbelievably grateful.

Riley loved all of it. And she was completely in her ele-ment as the center of attention. Hannah was happy to remain in the background, making sure everything was proceeding as it should, but Michael made a point of introducing "Riley's nanny and party planner" to everyone she hadn't yet met. There was nothing incorrect in that designation, and it wasn't like she expected or even wanted him to announce that they were lovers. But she wished he'd at least given a hint that she meant something more to him than the roles she filled in his daughter's life.

That tiny disappointment aside, she really enjoyed meeting his family. She already knew his sister, of course, and was pleased when Marissa jumped right in to help keep things running smoothly. She was introduced to Prince Cameron, his very pregnant wife, Gabriella, and their daughter, Sierra. The teenage princess was stunningly beautiful and surprisingly unaffected by her recently newfound status as a royal, happily jumping in to help the kids at the craft table.

She also met Rowan, the prince regent, his wife, Lara, and their sons Matthew and William; Prince Eric and Princess Molly and their kids, Maggie and Josh; Prince Christian—next in line to the throne—his sister, Alexandria, and their younger brother, Damon. Even Prince Marcus, who divided his time between Tesoro del Mar and West Virginia, happened to be in the country with his wife, Jewel, and their two daughters, Isabella and Rosalina, so they were able to attend.

They were all warm and welcoming, but it was their interactions with one another that Hannah observed just a little enviously. It had nothing to do with them being royal and everything to do with the obvious closeness they shared. As an only child, she'd never known anything to compare to that kind of absolute acceptance and unquestioning loyalty, but she was glad that Riley did.

As for Riley's "Grandmama"—well, Hannah didn't get any warm and fuzzy feelings from her, so she just kept a careful distance between them. And she succeeded, until she went into the house to tell Caridad that they were getting low on punch. On her way back out, the princess royal cornered her in the hall.

"I'll bet this party was your idea," she said.

And so was adding your name to the guest list, Hannah wanted to tell her. But she bit her tongue. Elena Leandres might be insufferably rude, but she was the princess royal and, as such, was entitled to deference if not respect.

"Riley doesn't need to play at being a princess," the birthday girl's grandmama continued. "She *is* one. And this whole display is tacky and inappropriate."

"I'm sorry you're not enjoying yourself."

The older woman's eyes narrowed on her. "But you are, aren't you?"

"I can't deny that I like a good party, Your Highness," she said unapologetically.

"Is it the party or the fairy tale?" she challenged. "Do you have some kind of fantasy in your mind that you're going to ride off into the sunset with the prince?"

"I have no illusions," she assured the prince's mother.

"I'm pleased to hear that, because although my son might lack sense and discretion in his choice of lovers, he would never tarnish his beloved wife's memory or his daughter's future by marrying someone like you."

One side of Elena's mouth curled in a nasty smile as Hannah's cheeks filled with color. "Did you really think I wouldn't guess the nature of your relationship with my son? I know what a man's thinking when he looks at a woman the way Michael looks at you—and it's not about hearts and flowers, it's about sex, pure and simple."

She forced herself to shrug, as if the princess royal's words hadn't cut to the quick. "Sure," she agreed easily. "But at least it's really great sex. And while this has been a fascinating conversation, I have to get back outside."

"You have not been dismissed," Elena snapped at her.

"I beg your pardon, Your Highness," she said through

clenched teeth. "But the children will be getting hungry and I promised Caridad that I would help serve lunch."

"Well, go on then," the princess royal smirked. "I wouldn't want to keep you from your duties."

And with those words and a dismissive wave of her hand, she quickly and efficiently put the nanny in her place.

Hannah's feelings were in turmoil as she headed up the stairs to her own room. She was angry and frustrated, embarrassed that her own thoughts and feelings had been so transparent, and her heart was aching because she knew that what the princess royal had said was true.

Not that she believed her relationship with the prince was about nothing more than sex. They had fun together and they'd become friends. But she also knew that while Michael had chosen to be with her now, he'd made no mention of a future for them together. And she had to wonder if maybe one of the reasons he'd chosen to get involved with her—aside from the obvious convenience—was because he could be confident that their relationship already had a predetermined expiration date. At the end of the summer, she would be leaving. The time they'd spent together was an interlude, that was all, and she'd been a fool to ever let herself hope it might be more.

Marissa was coming down the stairs as she was going up, and the princess's quick smile faded when she got close enough to see the distress that Hannah knew was likely etched on her face.

"Riley asked me to find you," she said. "She said she's absolutely starving and wanted to know when it would be time to eat."

"Please tell her that I'll be out in just a minute, Your Highness." She was anxious now to move things along and get this party over with, but she needed a few minutes alone to regain her composure before she could face anyone. And especially before she could face Michael.

"Hannah." The princess touched her arm, halting her progress. "I just saw my mother walk out—did she say something to upset you?"

"Of course not."

But it was obvious that Marissa didn't believe her, and that she was disappointed by the obvious lie.

"I thought we were becoming friends," she said gently.

Hannah looked away so that the princess wouldn't see the tears that stung her eyes. "You've been very kind to me, Your Highness, but—"

"Will you stop 'Your Highnessing' me," Marissa demanded, "and tell me what she said to you."

"It wasn't anything that wasn't true," Hannah finally acknowledged.

The princess sighed. "I'm not going to make excuses for her. All I can say is that she's so unhappy, her only pleasure comes from making others feel the same way."

"I'm not unhappy," Hannah assured her. She was simply resigned to the realities of her relationship with the prince, but also determined. If they only had two more weeks together, then she was going to cherish every moment.

"Actually, there is one more thing I'd like to say," Marissa told her.

"What's that?"

"That you're the best thing that has happened to my brother in a long time, so please don't let my mother—or anyone else—make you question what you have together."

Despite Marissa's reassurances, the rest of the day was bittersweet for Hannah, her happiness tempered by the realization that she wouldn't be around to witness the celebration of Riley's fifth birthday. She was only going to be at Cielo del Norte with the prince and his daughter for another two weeks. After that, they would return to their home in Verde Colinas, and she would go back to her apartment in town and her job at the high school, and she knew that she was going to miss them both unbearably.

She tried not to dwell on that fact, and when everyone joined together to sing "Happy Birthday," it was a welcome diversion. Caridad had offered to make the cake, as she had for each of the princess's previous birthdays, and Riley was stunned by the three-dimensional fairy-tale castle confection that she'd created, complete with towers and spires and even a drawbridge.

After everyone had their fill of cake and ice cream, Riley opened her gifts. She enthused over all of them, showing as much appreciation for the Little Miss Tennis visor that Kevin gave her to the elaborate back-to-school wardrobe from her aunt Marissa. Of course, her absolute favorite gift was the *Yo Gabba Gabba* CD collection from Grace, and she insisted on putting on the music for the enjoyment of all her guests.

The prince had given his gift to his daughter at breakfast: a three-story dollhouse, which she had absolutely adored. Partly because it came with dozens of pieces of furniture, but mostly because it was from her beloved daddy.

Hannah had walked the mall in San Pedro three times looking for something special for the little girl. She didn't want it to be anything showy or expensive, just something that might remind Riley of the time they'd spent together after she was gone. She finally found it in a little boutique that sold an indescribable variety of items ranging from handmade lace and estate jewelry to the latest in kitchen gadgets and children's toys. At first, it caught her eye just because it was funky and fun: a three-foot-long stuffed caterpillar with a purple body and high-top running shoes on its dozens of feet. Then when she picked it up, she noted the name on the tag: EMME.

"It's a palindrome!" Riley exclaimed happily.

"It looks like a caterpillar to me," her father said.

Riley just rolled her eyes and shared a secret smile with Hannah.

Several hours later, after the guests had all gone home and the remnants of the party had been cleared away by the rental company, Riley's eyes were closed. Even when Michael touched his lips to her cheek, she didn't stir.

"She's sleeping," he confirmed.

"She had a busy day," Hannah noted.

"A fabulous day—thanks to you."

"I tried not to go too over the top," she said.

His brows rose. "You don't think it was over the top?"

"I nixed the suggested arrival of the birthday girl in the horse-drawn glass carriage," she told him.

"I'm in awe of your restraint," he said dryly. "But truthfully, whatever it costs, it was worth every penny. I've never seen her so happy."

"Now I'm regretting that I didn't get the carriage."

"Then what would we do next year?"

She knew he'd only meant to tease her with the suggestion that this party couldn't be topped, but the words were a reminder to both of them that there was no *we* and Hannah wouldn't be around for the princess's next birthday.

"Brigitte called today," he said, in what seemed to Hannah a deliberate attempt to shift the direction of the conversation. "To wish Riley a happy birthday."

"That was thoughtful," she said. "How is she adjusting to life in Iceland?"

"Not easily."

"Does she want to come back?"

He laughed. "No. As much as she's struggling with culture shock, she is very much in love with her new husband."

"Then what is it that you're not telling me?" Because she was sure that he was holding something back.

"She did ask if I'd found a full-time nanny," he admitted. "And when I said I had not, she suggested that I interview her friend Margaux for the position."

Hannah had to remind herself that this wasn't unexpected. She'd known all along that the prince would be hiring a new nanny because she was leaving at the end of August. "Why do you sound as if that's a problem?" she asked.

"Because I was hoping that I might convince you to stay beyond the summer."

Her heart pounded hard against her ribs. This was what she hadn't even realized she wanted—what she hadn't dared let herself hope for. "You want me to stay?"

"You've been so wonderful with Riley, and she's going to be devastated if you leave."

Disappointment washed the roots of barely blossomed hope from her heart. "She'll be fine," she said, confident that it was true. The child had already proven that she was both adaptable and resilient. It was her own heart that gave Hannah concern, because she knew that when she left Cielo del Norte, she would be leaving the largest part of it behind.

"Okay, maybe the truth is that I'm not yet ready to let you go," Michael acknowledged.

Not yet ready—but he would be. Neither of them had any expectations of anything permanent or even long-term. At least none that she was willing to admit to him now. "We still have two weeks before the end of the summer," she said lightly.

"What if I'm not ready then, either?"

She didn't know what to say, how to answer his question in a way that wouldn't give away the feelings in her own heart. Because the truth was, she didn't want him to ever let her go—she wanted him to love her as much as she loved him, and she knew that wasn't going to happen.

He was still in love with Riley's mother, and even if he wasn't, she knew he wouldn't ever love her. Not enough.

Her father hadn't loved her enough to keep her with him, and Harrison hadn't loved her enough to defy his parents. And if she wasn't good enough for the heir of some obscure earldom, there was no way anyone would ever consider her good enough for a Tesorian prince. The princess royal had made that more than clear.

"Let's not think about that right now," she said, leading the way across the hall.

So long as they had tonight, she wasn't going to think about tomorrow.

Afterward, Hannah would wonder how it happened, because she knew she didn't consciously speak the words aloud. She certainly hadn't intended to tell him of the feelings that filled her heart. But when he pulled her close, tucking her against the warmth of his body so that she felt secure and cherished in his embrace, her emotions overruled reason. And as she started to drift toward slumber, the words slipped from between her lips as if of their own accord.

"I love you, Michael."

His only response was silence. She wanted to believe that he was already asleep and that he probably hadn't heard her impulsive confession, but the sudden tension that filled his body proved otherwise. The muscles in the arm that was wrapped around her grew taut, and she felt the sting of tears in her eyes.

She hadn't intended to confide her feelings. She knew she would be leaving her heart at Cielo del Norte but she'd hoped to at least take her pride. But keeping the feelings to herself certainly hadn't diminished them, and she was through pretending.

She did love him—with her whole heart. And she loved Riley as if the little girl was her own child. But accepting the truth of her feelings forced her to accept the more painful truths that were equally evident: there was no place for her here, and no future for her with the prince and his daughter.

Once again, she was trying to fit in someplace where she could never belong.

Chapter Sixteen

The night after Hannah's whispered declaration of her feelings, Michael didn't go to her room. It was the first time since their first night together that he'd gone directly to his big, empty bed. He didn't sleep well. He wasn't even sure that he'd slept at all.

But he knew he was doing the right thing. To continue to be with Hannah when he didn't—couldn't—feel the same way she did wasn't fair to either of them.

It was on Tuesday, after two restless, sleepless nights, that she knocked on his office door.

"Excuse me for interrupting, Your Highness, but I was wondering if I could have a minute of your time."

He cringed at the formal tone of her voice, hating the distance between them. He wanted to hear her speak his name, not his title. He wanted to take her in his arms and hold her so close that he could feel her heart beating against his. He wanted to touch his mouth to hers, to feel her lips yield to his kiss. But he had no right to want anything from her anymore.

"Of course, Hannah," he responded to her request.

"I got a notice from St. Eugene's that I'll be teaching a new course in the fall, and I was hoping to go back to Port Augustine at the end of this week."

This wasn't at all what he'd expected. He wasn't ready for her to leave, and he had no intention of letting her go. She had agreed to stay until the end of summer, to take care of his daughter.

"What about Riley?" he demanded now. "How can you just abandon her?"

"I'm not going anywhere until you've found someone else to take care of her."

"And what if I don't find anyone else?" he challenged.

He wasn't sure why he was fighting her on this. It was only seven days, and even if he didn't have anyone else by then, he would be happy to spend more time with his daughter during that last week. He didn't need a nanny, but he needed Hannah.

He wasn't sure where that last thought had come from— or how it could simultaneously feel so right and make him break out in a cold sweat.

"Margaux has agreed to come for an interview tomorrow."

"You're so eager to get away from here that you called her to set this up?"

"No," she denied. "Margaux called here, on Brigitte's advice, to set a date and time to meet with you. I just took the message."

"You could have said that I would get in touch with her when I returned to Port Augustine," he countered.

She looked at him oddly, as if she heard the note of desperation he tried to keep out of his voice. But all she said was, "I thought you would want this settled before then—to make sure Riley will be in good hands when you go back."

He couldn't refute the logic in that. Instead, he asked, "Is there nothing I can say to make you stay?"

She hesitated for a moment, as if considering her response, then finally said, "You really don't need me anymore. You and Riley are going to be just fine."

"Have you told her that you're leaving?"

"She won't be surprised. She knows I have to go back to my real job."

Just as he'd known it was only a temporary assignment when he'd hired her, so why was he fighting it now?

"I'll let you know after I meet with Margaux tomorrow," he told her.

"Thank you," she said.

And then she was gone.

Hannah was transferring her clothing from the dresser to her suitcase when Riley came into her room.

"Who's that lady with Daddy?" she demanded. "Is it true that she's going to be my new nanny?"

"That's for your daddy to decide," Hannah told her.

The princess crawled up onto Hannah's bed and hugged her knees to her chest. "Why don't I get to decide?"

"Because you're four."

"That's not my fault."

Hannah tousled her hair and smiled gently. "It's not a question of fault, it's just the way it is."

Riley watched as she continued to fill the suitcase. Hannah forced herself to concentrate on carefully arranging each item, because she knew that if she looked at the little girl right now, she would fall apart.

After a few minutes, Riley spoke in a quiet voice, "I don't want you to go."

Hannah's throat was tight, her eyes burning with unshed

tears. She drew in a deep breath and settled onto the edge of the bed, trying to find the words that would make goodbye easier for both of them.

But as soon as she sat down, Riley scooted over to wrap her arms around her, squeezing her so tight that the dam that was holding back Hannah's tears began to crack.

"I don't want to go, either," she admitted. "But we both knew that I was only going to be here for the summer."

"The summer's not over yet," the princess pointed out.

She rested her chin on top of the little girl's head, so Riley wouldn't see the tears that slid down her cheeks. "No, but it's getting close."

After another few minutes, Riley asked, "Can I come visit you?"

Hannah knew it would be best to make a clean break, to walk away from Cielo del Norte and never look back, but there was no way she could deny the child's request. "That's up to your dad, but if he says yes, it's absolutely okay with me."

"When?" Riley demanded.

The characteristic impatience in her voice made Hannah smile through her tears. "Anytime."

Margaux was everything Brigitte promised she would be. She was compassionate and knowledgeable and professional, and though his daughter kept insisting that she didn't want a new nanny, Michael remembered that she'd been equally resistant to Hannah at first. So he offered her the job, and she accepted. And when she agreed that she could start right away, he released Hannah from her obligation to stay until the end of the month.

It seemed pointless to have Margaux move into the beach house only to have to move back to the city a week later, so he decided that he and Riley might as well return to Verde Colinas early. Maybe his excuses were just that—certainly

Caridad thought so—and maybe it was true that he didn't want anyone else in Hannah's room. Not yet, while the memories were still fresh. By next summer, he was confident that he would be able to think of it as simply the nanny's room again and not think about all the hours that he'd spent in there with Hannah, talking and laughing with her, and making love with her.

Back in the city, Riley seemed to settle into her new routines fairly easily. Since summer was almost over, he'd started some of her lessons again, but on a much more modest scale. His daughter was polite and attentive to her teachers, and she cooperated willingly enough with Margaux, but still, something didn't seem quite right.

It took him almost a week to realize why the house seemed so somber and silent. Because not once in that entire time, not once in the six days since Hannah had been gone, did he hear his daughter laugh.

When she unpacked at home, Riley put the doll that Sam had given her back in its special place on the shelf. The silly stuffed caterpillar that Hannah had given to her as a birthday gift went on the bed, and Riley slept with it hugged close to her chest every night.

He wished that he could comfort his daughter, but he missed Hannah as much as she did. Maybe he hadn't sent her away, but he knew that he was responsible for her leaving just the same. She'd told him that she loved him, and he hadn't dared speak of the feelings that were in his own heart. Because he hadn't been willing to admit them, even to himself.

Now that she was gone, he could no longer deny the truth. Hannah hadn't just shown him how to build a better relationship with his daughter, she'd helped him heal and gave him hope for the future—a future he now knew that he wanted to share with her.

* * *

During the first week after her return from Cielo del Norte, Hannah missed Riley so much that she actually felt a pain in her chest whenever she thought of the little girl. As for the prince—well, she didn't even dare let herself think of the man who had stolen her heart.

She kept herself busy. She washed curtains and scrubbed floors; she repainted the walls and bought new throw rugs and cushions. She knew what she was doing: trying to make a fresh start. She wasn't sure that her plan would actually succeed, but she'd realized that the only way she could sleep at night was to fall into bed completely physically exhausted.

After everything was cleaned and painted and rearranged, she carted all of her boxes out of storage and back into her apartment. As she unpacked her belongings, she was amazed to think that only two months had passed since she'd packed it all away. It really wasn't a lot of time, but so much in her life had changed during that period. She had changed.

But she was doing okay—until she got a letter from Caridad. The housekeeper just wanted to let her know that Loretta had finally had her baby—almost two weeks late—and that she and Estavan were the proud grandparents of another beautiful baby girl.

Hannah was genuinely thrilled for them, and she sent a card and a gift for the baby. She'd considered hand-delivering the items, but decided against it. The memories were still too fresh, her heartache still too raw. She did hope to keep in touch with Caridad, as the housekeeper had become a wonderful friend, but there was no reason for her to ever go back to Cielo del Norte.

No reason except that she'd left her heart with Prince Michael while she'd been there. It didn't seem to matter that he didn't want it; she knew that it would always belong to him.

So many times, she thought back to that last conversation

in his office, when he'd asked, "Is there nothing I can say to make you stay?" And she'd wondered if anything might have been different if she'd had the courage to speak the words that had immediately come to mind: *Tell me you love me.*

But she knew that even if he had actually said those words to her, she wouldn't believe them. Because actions spoke louder than words, and he'd already made his feelings clear. She'd told him that she loved him—and he didn't even give her the lame I-care-about-you-but-I'm-not-ready-for-a-serious-relationship speech. He'd said nothing at all.

Still, she knew the mistake wasn't in speaking of the feelings that were in her heart; the mistake was in letting herself fall in love with a man that she'd known all along could never love her back. But even that knowledge didn't stop her from missing the prince and his little girl.

She was grateful when school started up again in September. She was anxious to get back into the familiar routines, confident that a return to her normal life would help her forget about Michael and Riley and how much she missed both of them.

Still, she thought about contacting him. Every day, she experienced moments of such intense yearning that she was tempted to pick up the phone, not just to hear his voice but to check on Riley. If she did, maybe he would give her permission to visit the little girl, but in the end she decided that wouldn't be a good idea for either of them. Margaux was the princess's nanny now, and she deserved a chance to bond with the child without Hannah in the way.

She was confident that Riley would adjust to these new changes in her life without much difficulty. She truly was an amazing child, and Hannah just hoped that the prince didn't fill her schedule with so many lessons and classes again that she forgot to be a child.

Instead of contacting the prince, Hannah busied herself working on new lesson plans for the current term. She was rereading the first play for her freshman drama class when there was a knock at the door Saturday afternoon. She was feeling desperate enough for a distraction that she responded to the summons. If it was a vacuum cleaner salesman, she might even invite him in to do a demonstration in the hope that it would possibly give her a half-hour reprieve from her thoughts of Michael and Riley.

But when she opened the door, she realized that there wasn't going to be any reprieve—because the prince and his daughter were standing in her hall.

"Hello, Hannah."

She opened her mouth, but no sound came out. She didn't know what to say—whether to invite them inside or send them away. And she was afraid that whatever choice she made would only result in fresh heartache.

"You said I could come visit, remember?" Riley's smile was uncharacteristically tentative, as if she was unsure of her welcome.

Hannah managed a smile, though she felt as if her heart was splitting wide open inside of her chest. "Of course I remember."

"Can we come in?" the prince asked.

She wished she could say no. And if his daughter wasn't standing at his side, she would have refused. But there was no way she could close the door now.

She stepped back so that they could enter, while questions swirled through her mind. Why were they here? Why now? Subconsciously, she touched a hand to her brow. The scar above her eye had started to fade, but the wounds on her heart were still raw and bleeding.

"Hannah?" the princess prompted, her little brow furrowed with concern.

She dropped her hand away, forced a smile. "Can I get you anything?"

She wasn't sure what to offer—her mind had gone blank

when she'd seen them standing outside of her door and she honestly couldn't remember what was in her refrigerator.

"Not for me, thanks," the prince said.

Riley shook her head.

Hannah led them into the living room. As a result of all of the cleaning and painting and redecorating, she knew the apartment looked good. Hardly up to royal standards, but then again, she wasn't a royal.

"So—were you just in the neighborhood?" she asked, attempting a casualness she wasn't feeling.

"No, Riley wanted to see you." Michael tucked his hands into his pockets. "Actually, we both wanted to see you."

"We miss you," the little girl said.

"How is school?" she asked Riley, forcing a note of cheerfulness into her voice even as her heart cracked wide open.

"It's okay," the princess said.

"Have you made lots of new friends?"

"A few."

Hannah swallowed. "And everything's going well...with the new nanny?"

The little girl looked at her daddy, as if deferring the question to him.

"Margaux is...almost perfect," he said.

"That's great," she said, and hoped that she sounded sincere.

"Almost," Riley repeated.

"Is there a problem?" Hannah asked, genuinely concerned.

"The only problem," Michael said, "is that she isn't you."

"We want you to come back," Riley said.

"This isn't fair," Hannah said to the prince, glaring at him through the sheen of tears that filled her eyes. "You can't bring your daughter here to—"

"It was Riley's idea," he told her. "There was no way she was letting me come here without her."

"Please, Hannah." The princess looked at her, those big brown eyes beseeching.

Hannah could barely speak around the lump in her throat. "I'm not really a nanny," she reminded the little girl gently. "I'm a high school teacher."

"We both understand that," Michael assured her. "And the thing is, Riley and I had a long talk about it and agreed that, since she's in school now during the week anyway, she probably doesn't need a nanny."

"Then why are you here?"

"Because I do need a mcm," Riley piped up.

"And I need a wife," Michael said. "So—" The prince looked at his daughter, she gave him a quick nod, then they spoke in unison: "Will you marry us, Hannah?"

She could only stare at them both, her eyes filling with tears all over again.

Michael nudged his daughter.

"Oh." The little girl reached into the pocket of her skirt and pulled out a small box. She tried to flip open the lid, but it snapped shut again—catching her finger.

"Ow." Riley shook her hand free, and the box went flying across the floor, disappearing under the sofa.

Hannah had to laugh through her tears.

"This isn't quite how I imagined the scene playing out," Michael admitted.

It was a scene she hadn't dared let herself imagine and still wasn't entirely sure was real.

"Can you trust that I have a ring or do I have to dig the box out from under the furniture before you'll answer the question?" he asked.

"I don't care about the ring," she assured him.

"It's a really pretty ring," Riley said, making Hannah smile.

"But you're not saying anything," he prompted.

"I've got it, Daddy." The princess held up the box she'd

retrieved from beneath the sofa. Then she came over and opened it carefully so that Hannah could see the gorgeous princess-cut diamond solitaire set in a platinum band. "Now you're supposed to say yes."

She wanted to say yes. More than anything, she wanted to say yes, and it had nothing to do with the ring. It had to do with the fact that the prince was offering her everything she'd ever wanted and more than she'd ever dreamed of, but she felt as if they were both forgetting a couple important issues. "I'm a commoner, Michael."

"Which only means you don't carry all of the baggage that goes along with a title," he assured her.

"I realize it's not a big deal to you, but maybe it should be. And your mother—"

"Has absolutely no say in any of this," he said firmly.

"Daddy told Grandmama that if she can't accept you, then she can't be part of our family," Riley told her.

"You talked to your mother…about me?"

"I wanted her to know that I won't tolerate any more interference in my life," he said.

"I don't want to be the cause of any dissension in your relationship," she said, both surprised and humbled that he would take such a stand for her.

"You're not," Michael assured her. "If anything, confronting my mother about her attitude toward you gave me the opportunity to clear the air about a lot of things. I'm not naïve enough to believe that we came to any kind of understanding, but I am confident that she won't cause any problems for us ever again."

He spoke with such certainty, she couldn't help but believe him. But she had other—and even bigger—concerns than the princess royal.

"Needing a wife—and a mother for Riley—aren't the best reasons to get married," she said softly.

He smiled as he took both of her hands in his. "Did I

gloss over the I-love-you-more-than-I-ever-thought-it-was-possible-to-love-somebody part?"

Her heart swelled so much in response to his words that her chest actually ached with the effort to contain it. "Actually, you skipped it altogether."

"It's true," he told her. "I didn't plan to ever fall in love again. Truthfully, I didn't want to ever fall in love again."

"Because you still love Sam," she guessed.

"Sam will always have a place in my heart," he admitted, "because she was the first woman I ever loved and Riley's mother. But the rest of my heart is yours, for now and forever. So now the question I need answered is: do you love me?"

"You know I do."

"Is that a yes?" Riley wanted to know.

Hannah laughed. "That is very definitely a yes."

The princess clapped her hands together. "Now you have to put the ring on her finger, Daddy."

So he did.

"And kiss her."

And he did that, too.

He kissed her very tenderly and very thoroughly, until all of the loneliness and anguish of the past few weeks was forgotten because her heart was too full of love to feel anything else.

And still he continued to kiss her—until Riley pushed her way in between them.

"Are we married now?" she asked.

"Not quite yet," the prince said.

Riley sighed. "Can Hannah come home with us tonight anyway?"

"What do you say?" he asked, drawing her to her feet. "Will you come home with us tonight?"

Home.

She looked around at the apartment that had been her

residence for almost three years and felt absolutely no regret about leaving. It was only a collection of rooms—cold and empty without the man and the little girl she loved.

"There is nowhere else I want to be," she said truthfully.

"Just one more thing," Michael said.

"What's that?"

"If you ever retell the story of my proposal, will you edit out the awkward parts?" he asked.

She shook her head. "Absolutely not. I'm going to remember each tiny detail forever, because this moment—with you and Riley—is my every dream come true."

Epilogue

ROYAL WEDDING BELLS TOLL AGAIN
by Alex Girard

Last summer, Prince Michael Leandres was looking for a nanny for his young daughter and hired a high school teacher instead. At the time, it might have seemed that he'd made an error in judgment, but the lucky guests in attendance when the prince married Hannah Castillo at the Cathedral of Christ the King on Friday night would definitely disagree.

The ceremony began with four-and-a-half-year-old Princess Riley tossing white rose petals as she made her way down the aisle and toward the front of the church where her father, immaculately attired in a classic Armani tuxedo, was waiting. Then came the bride, in a strapless silk crepe sheath by Vera Wang, carrying a bouquet of calla lilies and freesia, proudly escorted by her uncle, Doctor Phillip Marotta.

Despite the more than two hundred people in the church,

the bride and the groom seemed to have eyes only for each other as they spoke traditional vows and exchanged rings. The couple then veered from convention by each reaching a hand to Princess Riley and drawing her into their circle, and the bride made a public promise to the groom's daughter that she would always be there for her, too, to guide her through good times and bad. The little girl chimed in to assert that they would all be good times, now that they were finally a family.

And when the bride and groom and his daughter lit the unity candle together, there wasn't anyone in the church who doubted that the young princess's words were true.

* * * * *

Harlequin®

COMING NEXT MONTH
Available October 25, 2011

#2149 CHRISTMAS IN COLD CREEK
RaeAnne Thayne
The Cowboys of Cold Creek

#2150 A BRAVO HOMECOMING
Christine Rimmer
Bravo Family Ties

#2151 A MAVERICK FOR CHRISTMAS
Leanne Banks
Montana Mavericks: The Texans Are Coming!

#2152 A COULTER'S CHRISTMAS PROPOSAL
Lois Faye Dyer
Big Sky Brothers

#2153 A BRIDE BEFORE DAWN
Sandra Steffen
Round-the-Clock Brides

#2154 MIRACLE UNDER THE MISTLETOE
Tracy Madison
The Foster Brothers

SPECIAL EDITION

REQUEST YOUR FREE BOOKS!

2 FREE NOVELS PLUS 2 FREE GIFTS!

♦ **Harlequin®**

SPECIAL EDITION

Life, Love & Family

YES! Please send me 2 FREE Harlequin® Special Edition novels and my 2 FREE gifts (gifts are worth about $10). After receiving them, if I don't wish to receive any more books, I can return the shipping statement marked "cancel." If I don't cancel, I will receive 6 brand-new novels every month and be billed just $4.49 per book in the U.S. or $5.24 per book in Canada. That's a saving of at least 14% off the cover price! It's quite a bargain! Shipping and handling is just 50¢ per book in the U.S. and 75¢ per book in Canada.* I understand that accepting the 2 free books and gifts places me under no obligation to buy anything. I can always return a shipment and cancel at any time. Even if I never buy another book, the two free books and gifts are mine to keep forever.

235/335 HDN FEGF

Name _____ (PLEASE PRINT) _____

Address _____ Apt. # _____

City _____ State/Prov. _____ Zip/Postal Code _____

Signature (if under 18, a parent or guardian must sign) _____

Mail to the **Reader Service:**
IN U.S.A.: P.O. Box 1867, Buffalo, NY 14240-1867
IN CANADA: P.O. Box 609, Fort Erie, Ontario L2A 5X3

Not valid for current subscribers to Harlequin Special Edition books.

Want to try two free books from another line?
Call 1-800-873-8635 or visit www.ReaderService.com.

* Terms and prices subject to change without notice. Prices do not include applicable taxes. Sales tax applicable in N.Y. Canadian residents will be charged applicable taxes. Offer not valid in Quebec. This offer is limited to one order per household. All orders subject to credit approval. Credit or debit balances in a customer's account(s) may be offset by any other outstanding balance owed by or to the customer. Please allow 4 to 6 weeks for delivery. Offer available while quantities last.

Your Privacy—The Reader Service is committed to protecting your privacy. Our Privacy Policy is available online at www.ReaderService.com or upon request from the Reader Service.

We make a portion of our mailing list available to reputable third parties that offer products we believe may interest you. If you prefer that we not exchange your name with third parties, or if you wish to clarify or modify your communication preferences, please visit us at www.ReaderService.com/consumerschoice or write to us at Reader Service Preference Service, P.O. Box 9062, Buffalo, NY 14269. Include your complete name and address.

HSE11B

On impulse, he unfolded himself from the bar stool. "Need
a hand?"

"Thank you! I…" She lifted her gaze from the floor to
his jeans and then raised her eyes. When she identified him
her hazel eyes turned from grateful to unfriendly and cold,
as if he'd somehow thrown the broken glasses at her head.

He also thought he saw a glimmer of panic in those
interesting depths, which instantly stirred his curiosity like
cream swirling through coffee.

"I've got it, Officer. Thank you." Her voice was several
degrees colder than the whirl of sleet outside the windows.

Despite her protests, he knelt down beside her and began
to pick up shards of broken glass. "No problem. Those trays
can be slippery."

This close, he picked up the scent of her, something fresh
and flowery that made him think of a mountain meadow on
a July afternoon. She had a soft, lush mouth and for one
brief, insane moment, he wanted to push aside that stray lock

of hair slipping from her ponytail and taste her. Apparently he needed to spend a lot less time working and a great deal *more* time recreating with the opposite sex if he could have sudden random fantasies about a woman he wasn't even inclined to like, pretty or not.

"I'm Trace Bowman. You must be new in town."

She didn't answer immediately and he could almost see the wheels turning in her head. Why the hesitancy? And why that little hint of unease he could see clouding the edge of her gaze? His presence was obviously making her uncomfortable and Trace couldn't help wondering why.

"Yes. We've been here a few weeks."

"Well, I'm just up the road about four lots, in the white house with the cedar shake roof, if you or your daughter need anything." He smiled at her as he picked up the last shard of glass and set it on her tray.

Definitely a story there, he thought as she hurried away. He just might need to dig a little into her background to find out why someone with fine clothes and nice jewelry, and who so obviously didn't have experience as a waitress, would be here slinging hash at The Gulch. Was she running away from someone? A bad marriage?

So…Rebecca Parsons. Not Becky. An intriguing woman. It had been a long time since one of those had crossed his path here in Pine Gulch.

Trace won't rest until he finds out Rebecca's secret, but will he still have that same attraction to her once he does? Find out in CHRISTMAS IN COLD CREEK. Available November 2011 from Harlequin® Special Edition®.

Harlequin
Super Romance

*Discover a fresh, heartfelt new romance
from acclaimed author*

Sarah Mayberry

Businessman Flynn Randall's life is
complicated. So he doesn't need the
distraction of fun, spontaneous Mel Porter.
But he can't stop thinking about her. Maybe
he can handle one more complication....

All They Need

*Available November 8, 2011,
wherever books are sold!*